PRAISE FOR
THE GIRL WHO LOVED TOM GORDON

'Its streamlined plot is unremitting . . . A compelling battle for survival that you dare not put down' – *Daily Mail*

'Vintage King . . . the quality of the prose is consistently impressive and his trump card is his ability to arouse empathy for the plight of his young heroine' – *Independent on Sunday*

'Moving, gripping. One of his best . . . A literary home run' – *Daily Mirror*

PRAISE FOR
THE GIRL WHO LOVED TOM GORDON

'Utterly compulsive bears ample witness to King's mastery of his craft' – *Mail on Sunday*

'Part adventure, part modern allegory, this is King writing at his compelling best' – *Sunday Express*

'The story of [Trisha McFarland] coming to terms with her predicament and of her indomitable spirit make this one of King's most subtle spine tinglers' – *Birmingham Evening Mail*

'NOTHING
CAN LIVE
UP TO THE
MEMORY
OF A GOOD
SCARE.'

STEPHEN
KING

ROSE MADDER

After fourteen years, Rosie Daniels flees from her abusive husband. But Norman Daniels, a police officer, uses his law-enforcement connections to track his wayward wife.

FULL DARK, NO STARS

Is it possible to fully know anyone? Even those we love the most? What does it take to tip someone over the edge to commit a crime?

'Fine stories to take with us into the night' – Neil Gaiman, *Guardian*

By Stephen King and published by Hodder & Stoughton

STEPHEN KING

THE GIRL WHO LOVED TOM GORDON

HODDER

Grateful acknowledgement is made to Dennis V. Drinkwater of Giant
Glass for permission to reprint the Giant Glass commercial jingle.
Lyrics from 'Gotta Get Next to You (Jus' Slip Me a Taste)' by Richie
'Records' Tozier, copyright 1998 Soul Fine Music. Used by permission

First published in Great Britain in 1987 by Hodder & Stoughton
An Hachette UK company

This paperback edition published in 2019

The right of Stephen King to be identified as the Author
of the Work has been asserted by him in accordance with the
Copyright, Designs and Patents Act 1988

A Hodder Paperback

1

A CIP catalogue record for this title is
available from the British Library

ISBN 978 1 529 31112 9

Typeset by Rowland Phototypesetting Ltd,
Bury St Edmunds, Suffolk
Printed and bound by Clays Ltd, Elcograf S.p.A.

Hodder & Stoughton policy is to use papers that are natural,
renewable and recyclable products and made from wood grown
in sustainable forests. The logging and manufacturing processes
are expected to conform to the environmental regulations
of the country of origin

Hodder & Stoughton
Carmelite House
50 Victoria Embankment
London EC4Y 0DZ

www.hodder.co.uk

This is for my son Owen,
who ended up teaching me a lot more
about the game of baseball than I ever taught him.

JUNE 1998

PREGAME

The world had teeth and it could bite you with them anytime it wanted. Trisha McFarland discovered this when she was nine years old. At ten o'clock on a morning in early June she was sitting in the back seat of her mother's Dodge Caravan, wearing her blue Red Sox batting practice jersey (the one with 36 GORDON on the back) and playing with Mona, her doll. At ten thirty she was lost in the woods. By eleven she was trying not to be terrified, trying not to let herself think, *This is serious, this is very serious.* Trying not to think that sometimes when people got lost in the woods they got seriously hurt. Sometimes they died.

All because I needed to pee, she thought . . . except she hadn't needed to pee all that badly, and in any case she could have asked Mom and Pete to wait up the trail a minute while she went behind a tree. They were fighting again, gosh what a surprise *that* was, and that was why she had dropped behind a little bit, and without saying anything. That was why she had stepped off the trail and behind a high stand of bushes. She needed a breather, simple as that. She was tired of listening to them argue, tired of trying to sound bright and cheerful, close to screaming at her mother, *Let him go, then! If he wants to go back to Malden and live with Dad so much, why don't you just let him? I'd drive him myself if I had a license, just to get some peace and quiet around here!* And what then? What would her mother say then? What kind of look would come over her face? And Pete. He was older, almost fourteen, and not stupid, so why didn't he know better? Why couldn't he just give it a rest? *Cut the crap* was what she wanted to say to him (to both of them, really), *just cut the crap*.

The divorce had happened a year ago, and their mother had gotten custody. Pete had protested the move from suburban Boston to southern Maine bitterly and at length. Part of it really was wanting to be with Dad, and that was the lever he always used on Mom (he understood with some unerring instinct that it was the one he could plant the deepest and pull on the hardest), but Trisha knew it wasn't the only reason, or even the biggest one. The real reason Pete wanted out was that he hated Sanford Middle School.

In Malden he'd had it pretty well whipped. He'd run the computer club like it was his own private kingdom; he'd had friends – nerds, yeah, but they went around in a group and the bad kids didn't pick on them. At Sanford Middle there *was* no computer club and he'd only made a single friend, Eddie Rayburn. Then in January Eddie moved away, also the victim of a parental breakup. That made Pete a loner, anyone's game. Worse, a lot of kids laughed at him. He had picked up a nickname which he hated: Pete's CompuWorld.

On most of the weekends when she and Pete didn't go down to Malden to be with their father, their mother took them on outings. She was grimly dedicated to these, and although Trisha wished with all her heart that Mom would stop – it was on the outings that the worst fights happened

4

– she knew that wasn't going to happen. Quilla Andersen (she had taken back her maiden name and you could bet Pete hated that, too) had the courage of her convictions. Once, while staying at the Malden house with Dad, Trisha had heard their father talking to his own Dad on the phone. 'If Quilla had been at Little Big Horn, the Indians would have lost,' he said, and although Trisha didn't like it when Dad said stuff like that about Mom – it seemed babyish as well as disloyal – she couldn't deny that there was a nugget of truth in that particular observation.

Over the last six months, as things grew steadily worse between Mom and Pete, she had taken them to the auto museum in Wiscasset, to the Shaker Village in Gray, to The New England Plant-A-Torium in North Wyndham, to Six-Gun City in Randolph, New Hampshire, on a canoe trip down the Saco River, and on a skiing trip to Sugarloaf (where Trisha had sprained her ankle, an injury over which her mother and father had later had a screaming fight; what fun divorce was, what really good fun).

Sometimes, if he really liked a place, Pete would give his mouth a rest. He had pronounced Six-Gun City 'for babies,' but Mom had allowed him to spend most of the visit in the room where the electronic games were, and Pete had gone home not exactly happy but at least silent. On the other hand, if Pete didn't like one of the places their Mom picked (his least favorite by far had been the Plant-A-Torium; returning to Sanford that day he had been in an especially boogery frame of mind), he was generous in sharing his opinion. 'Go along to get along' wasn't in his nature. Nor was it in their mother's, Trisha supposed. She herself thought it was an excellent philosophy, but of course everyone took one look at her and pronounced her her father's child. Sometimes that bothered her, but mostly she liked it.

Trisha didn't care *where* they went on Saturdays, and would have been perfectly happy with a steady diet of amusement parks and mini-golf courses just because they minimized the increasingly horrible arguments. But Mom wanted the trips to be instructive, too – hence the Plant-A-Torium and Shaker Village. On top of his other problems, Pete resented having education rammed down his throat on Saturdays, when he would rather have been up in his room, playing Sanitarium or Riven on his Mac. Once or twice he had shared his opinion ('This sucks!' pretty well summed it up) so generously that Mom had sent him back to the car and told him to sit there and 'compose himself' until she and Trisha came back.

Trisha wanted to tell Mom she was wrong to treat him like he was a kindergartener who needed a time-out – that someday they'd come back to the van and find it empty, Pete having decided to hitchhike back to Massachusetts – but of course she said nothing. The Saturday outings themselves were wrong, but Mom would never accept that. By the end of some of them Quilla Andersen looked at least five years older than when they had set out, with deep lines grooved down the sides of her mouth and one hand constantly rubbing her temple, as if she had a headache . . . but she would still never stop. Trisha knew it. Maybe if her mother had been at Little Big Horn the Indians still would have won, but the body-count would have been considerably higher.

This week's outing was to an unincorporated township

in the western part of the state. The Appalachian Trail wound through the area on its way to New Hampshire. Sitting at the kitchen table the night before, Mom had shown them photos from a brochure. Most of the pictures showed happy hikers either striding along a forest trail or standing at scenic lookouts, shading their eyes and peering across great wooded valleys at the time-eroded but still formidable peaks of the central White Mountains.

Pete sat at the table, looking cataclysmically bored, refusing to give the brochure more than a glance. For her part, Mom had refused to notice his ostentatious lack of interest. Trisha, as was increasingly her habit, became brightly enthusiastic. These days she often sounded to herself like a contestant on a TV game show, all but peeing in her pants at the thought of winning a set of waterless cookware. And how did she *feel* to herself these days? Like glue holding together two pieces of something that was broken. *Weak* glue.

Quilla had closed the brochure and turned it over. On the back was a map. She tapped a snaky blue line. 'This is Route 68,' she said. 'We'll park the car here, in this parking lot.' She tapped a little blue square. Now she traced one finger along a snaky red line. 'This is the Appalachian Trail between Route 68 and Route 302 in North Conway, New Hampshire. It's only six miles, and rated Moderate. Well . . . this one little section in the middle is marked Moderate-to-Difficult, but not to the point where we'd need climbing gear or anything.'

She tapped another blue square. Pete was leaning his head on one hand, looking the other way. The heel of his palm had pulled the left side of his mouth up into a sneer.

He had started getting pimples this year and a fresh crop gleamed on his forehead. Trisha loved him, but sometimes – last night at the kitchen table, as Mom explained their route, for example – she hated him, too. She wanted to tell him to stop being a chicken, because that was what it came down to when you cut to the chase, as their Dad said. Pete wanted to run back to Malden with his little teenage tail between his legs because he was a chicken. He didn't care about Mom, didn't care about Trisha, didn't even care if being with Dad would be good for him in the long run. What Pete cared about was not having anyone to eat lunch with on the gym bleachers. What Pete cared about was that when he walked into homeroom after the first bell someone always yelled, 'Hey CompuWorld! Howya doon, homo-boy?'

'This is the parking lot where we come out,' Mom had said, either not noticing that Pete wasn't looking at the map or pretending not to. 'A van shows up there around three. It'll take us back around to our car. Two hours later we're home again, and I'll haul you guys to a movie if we're not too tired. How does that sound?'

Pete had said nothing last night, but he'd had plenty to say this morning, starting with the ride up from Sanford. He didn't want to do this, it was ultimately stupid, plus he'd heard it was going to rain later on, why did they have to spend a whole Saturday walking in the woods during the worst time of the year for bugs, what if Trisha got poison ivy (as if he cared), and on and on and on. Yatata-yatata-yatata. He even had the gall to say he should be home studying for his final exams. Pete had never studied on Saturday in his life, as far as Trisha knew. At first Mom

8

didn't respond, but finally he began getting under her skin. Given enough time, he always did. By the time they got to the little dirt parking area on Route 68, her knuckles were white on the steering wheel and she was speaking in clipped tones which Trisha recognized all too well. Mom was leaving Condition Yellow behind and going to Condition Red. It was looking like a very long six-mile walk through the western Maine woods, all in all.

At first Trisha had tried to divert them, exclaiming over barns and grazing horses and picturesque graveyards in her best oh-wow-it's-waterless-cookware voice, but they ignored her and after awhile she had simply sat in the back seat with Mona on her lap (her Dad liked to call Mona Moanie Balogna) and her knapsack beside her, listening to them argue and wondering if she herself might cry, or actually go crazy. Could your family fighting all the time drive you crazy? Maybe when her mother started rubbing her temples with the tips of her fingers, it wasn't because she had a headache but because she was trying to keep her brains from undergoing spontaneous combustion or explosive decompression, or something.

To escape them, Trisha opened the door to her favorite fantasy. She took off her Red Sox cap and looked at the signature written across the brim in broad black felt-tip strokes; this helped get her in the mood. It was Tom Gordon's signature. Pete liked Mo Vaughn, and their Mom was partial to Nomar Garciaparra, but Tom Gordon was Trisha's and her Dad's favorite Red Sox player. Tom Gordon was the Red Sox closer; he came on in the eighth or ninth inning when the game was close but the Sox were still on top. Her Dad admired Gordon because he never seemed to lose his nerve – 'Flash has got icewater in his veins,' Larry McFarland liked to say – and Trisha always said the same thing, sometimes adding that she liked Gordon because he had the guts to throw a curve on three-and-oh (this was something her father had read to her in a *Boston Globe* column). Only to Moanie Balogna and (once) to her girl-friend, Pepsi Robichaud, had she said more. She told Pepsi she thought Tom Gordon was 'pretty good-looking.' To Mona she threw caution entirely to the winds, saying that Number 36 was the handsomest man alive, and if he ever touched her hand she'd faint. If he ever kissed her, even on the cheek, she thought she'd probably die.

Now, as her mother and her brother fought in the front seat – about the outing, about Sanford Middle School, about their dislocated life – Trisha looked at the signed cap her Dad had somehow gotten her in March, just before the season started, and thought this:

I'm in Sanford Park, just walking across the playground to Pepsi's house on an ordinary day. And there's this guy standing at the hotdog wagon. He's wearing blue jeans and a white T-shirt and he's got a gold chain around his neck – he's got his back to me but I can see the chain winking in the sun. Then he turns around and I see . . . oh I can't believe it but it's true, it's really him, it's Tom Gordon, *why he's in Sanford is a mystery but it's him, all right, and oh God his eyes, just like when he's looking in for the sign with men on base, those eyes, and he smiles and says he's a little lost, he wonders if I know a town called North Berwick, how to get there, and oh God, oh my God I'm shaking, I won't be able to say a word, I'll open my mouth and nothing will come out but a little dry squeak, what Dad calls a mousefart, only when I try I can speak, I sound almost normal, and I say . . .*

I say, he says, then I say and then he says: thinking about how they might talk while the fighting in the front seat of the Caravan drew steadily farther away. (Sometimes, Trisha had decided, silence was life's greatest blessing.) She was still looking fixedly at the signature on the visor of her baseball cap when Mom turned into the parking area, still far away (*Trish is off in her own world* was how her father put it), unaware that there were teeth hidden in the ordinary texture of things and she would soon know it. She was in Sanford, not in TR-90. She was in the town park, not at an entry-point to the Appalachian Trail. She was with Tom Gordon, Number 36, and he was offering to buy her a hotdog in exchange for directions to North Berwick.

Oh, bliss.

FIRST INNING

Mom and Pete gave it a rest as they got their packs and Quilla's wicker plant-collection basket out of the van's back end; Pete even helped Trisha get her pack settled evenly on her back, tightening one of the straps, and she had a moment's foolish hope that now things were going to be all right.

'Kids got your ponchos?' Mom asked, looking up at the sky. There was still blue up there, but the clouds were thickening in the west. It very likely *would* rain, but probably not soon enough for Pete to have a satisfying whine about being soaked.

'I've got mine, Mom!' Trisha chirruped in her oh-boy-waterless-cookware voice.

Pete grunted something that might have been yes.

'Lunches?'

Affirmative from Trisha; another low grunt from Pete.

'Good, because I'm not sharing mine.' She locked the Caravan, then led them across the dirt lot toward a sign marked TRAIL WEST, with an arrow beneath. There were maybe a dozen other cars in the lot, all but theirs with out-of-state plates.

'Bug-spray?' Mom asked as they stepped onto the path leading to the trail. 'Trish?'

'Got it!' she chirruped, not entirely positive she did but not wanting to stop with her back turned so that Mom could have a rummage. That would get Pete going again for sure. If they kept walking, though, he might see something which would interest him, or at least distract him. A raccoon. Maybe a deer. A dinosaur would be good. Trisha giggled.

'What's funny?' Mom asked.

'Just me thinks,' Trisha replied, and Quilla frowned – 'me thinks' was a Larry McFarland-ism. *Well let her frown,* Trisha thought. *Let her frown all she wants. I'm with her, and I don't complain about it like old grouchy there, but he's still my Dad and I still love him.*

Trisha touched the brim of her signed cap, as if to prove it.

'Okay, kids, let's go,' Quilla said. 'And keep your eyes open.'

'I hate this,' Pete almost groaned – it was the first clearly articulated thing he'd said since they got out of the van, and Trisha thought: *Please God, send something. A deer or a dinosaur or a UFO. Because if You don't, they're going right back at it.*

God sent nothing but a few mosquito scouts that would no doubt soon be reporting back to the main army that fresh meat was on the move, and by the time they passed a sign reading NO. CONWAY STATION 5.5 MI., the two of them were at it full-bore again, ignoring the woods, ignoring her, ignoring everything but each other. Yatata-yatata-yatata. It was, Trisha thought, like some sick kind of making out.

It was a shame, too, because they were missing stuff that was actually pretty neat. The sweet, resiny smell of the pines, for instance, and the way the clouds seemed so close – less like clouds than like draggles of whitish-gray smoke.

She guessed you'd have to be an adult to call something as boring as walking one of your hobbies, but this really wasn't bad. She didn't know if the entire Appalachian Trail was as well-maintained as this – probably not – but if it was, she guessed she could understand why people with nothing better to do decided to walk all umpty-thousand miles of it. Trisha thought it was like walking on a broad, winding avenue through the woods. It wasn't paved, of course, and it ran steadily uphill, but it was easy enough walking. There was even a little hut with a pump inside it and a sign which read: WATER TESTS OK FOR DRINKING. PLEASE FILL PRIMER JUG FOR NEXT PERSON.

She had a bottle of water in her pack – a big one with a squeeze-top – but suddenly all Trisha wanted in the world was to prime the pump in the little hut and get a drink, cold and fresh, from its rusty lip. She would drink and pretend she was Bilbo Baggins, on his way to the Misty Mountains.

'Mom?' she asked from behind them. 'Could we stop long enough to—'

'Making friends is a *job*, Peter,' her mother was saying. She didn't look back at Trisha. 'You can't just stand around and wait for kids to come to you.'

'Mom? Pete? Could we please stop for just a—'

'You don't understand,' he said heatedly. 'You don't have a *clue*. I don't know how things were when you were in junior high, but they're a lot different now.'

'Pete? Mom? Mommy? There's a pump—' Actually there *was* a pump; that was now the grammatically correct way to put it, because the pump was behind them, and getting farther behind all the time.

15

'I don't accept that,' Mom said briskly, all business, and Trisha thought: *No wonder she drives him crazy.* Then, resentfully: *They don't even know I'm here. The Invisible Girl, that's me. I might as well have stayed home.* A mosquito whined in her ear and she slapped at it irritably.

They came to a fork in the trail. The main branch — not quite as wide as an avenue now, but still not bad — went off to the left, marked by a sign reading NO. CONWAY 5.2. The other branch, smaller and mostly overgrown, read KEZAR NOTCH 10.

'Guys, I have to pee,' said The Invisible Girl, and of course neither of them took any notice; they just headed up the branch which led to North Conway, walking side by side like lovers and looking into each other's faces like lovers and arguing like the bitterest enemies. *We should have stayed home,* Trisha thought. *They could have done this at home, and I could have read a book.* The Hobbit *again, maybe — a story about guys who like to walk in the woods.*

'Who cares, I'm peeing,' she said sulkily, and walked a little way down the path marked KEZAR NOTCH. Here the pines which had stayed modestly back from the main trail crowded in, reaching with their blueblack branches, and there was underbrush, as well — clogs and clogs of it. She looked for the shiny leaves that meant poison ivy, poison oak, or poison sumac, and didn't see any . . . thank God for small favors. Her mother had shown her pictures of those and taught her to identify them two years ago, when life had been happier and simpler. In those days Trisha had gone tramping in the woods with her mother quite a bit. (Pete's bitterest complaint about the trip to Plant-A-Torium was that their *mother* had wanted to go there. The

16

obvious truth of this seemed to blind him to how selfish he had sounded, harping on it all day long.)

On one of their walks, Mom had also taught her how girls peed in the woods. She began by saying, 'The most important thing – maybe the *only* important thing – is not to do it in a patch of poison ivy. Now look. Watch me and do it just the way I do it.'

Trisha now looked both ways, saw no one, and decided she'd get off the trail anyway. The way to Kezar Notch looked hardly used – little more than an alley compared to the broad thoroughfare of the main trail – but she still didn't want to squat right in the middle of it. It seemed indecorous.

She stepped off the path in the direction of the North Conway fork, and she could still hear them arguing. Later on, after she was good and lost and trying not to believe she might die in the woods, Trisha would remember the last phrase she got in the clear; her brother's hurt, indignant voice: – *don't know why we have to pay for what you guys did wrong!*

She walked half a dozen steps toward the sound of his voice, stepping carefully around a clump of brambles even though she was wearing jeans instead of shorts. She paused, looked back, and realized she could still see the Kezar Notch path ... which meant that anyone coming along it would be able to see *her*, squatting and peeing with a half-loaded knapsack on her back and a Red Sox cap on her head. Em-*bare-ASS*-ing, as Pepsi might say (Quilla Andersen had once remarked that Penelope Robichaud's picture should be next to the word *vulgar* in the dictionary).

17

Trisha went down a mild slope, her sneakers slipping a little in a carpet of last year's dead leaves, and when she got to the bottom she couldn't see the Kezar Notch path anymore. Good. From the other direction, straight ahead through the woods, she heard a man's voice and a girl's answering laughter – hikers on the main trail, and not far away, by the sound. As Trisha unsnapped her jeans it occurred to her that if her mother and brother paused in their oh-so-interesting argument, looking behind them to see how sis was doing, and saw a strange man and woman instead, they might be worried about her.

Good! Give them something else to think about for a few minutes. Something besides themselves.

The trick, her mother had told her on that better day in the woods two years ago, wasn't going outdoors – girls could do that every bit as well as boys – but to do it without soaking your clothes.

Trisha held onto the conveniently jutting branch of a nearby pine, bent her knees, then reached between her legs with her free hand, yanking her pants and her underwear forward and out of the firing line. For a moment nothing happened – wasn't that just typical – and Trish sighed. A mosquito whined bloodthirstily around her left ear, and she had no hand free with which to slap at it.

'Oh waterless cookware!' she said angrily, but it was funny, really quite deliciously stupid and funny, and she began to laugh. As soon as she started laughing she started peeing. When she was done she looked around dubiously for something to blot with and decided – once more it was her father's phrase – not to push her luck. She gave her tail a little shake (as if that would really do any good)

18

and then yanked up her pants. When the mosquito buzzed the side of her face again, she slapped it briskly and looked with satisfaction at the small bloody smear in the cup of her palm. 'Thought I was unloaded, partner, didn't you?' she said.

Trisha turned back toward the slope, and then turned around again as the worst idea of her life came to her. This idea was to go forward instead of backtracking to the Kezar Notch trail. The paths had forked in a Y; she would simply walk across the gap and rejoin the main trail. Piece of cake. There was no chance of getting lost, because she could hear the voices of the other hikers so clearly. There was really no chance of getting lost at all.

SECOND INNING

The west side of the ravine in which Trisha had taken her rest-stop was considerably steeper than the side she had come down. She climbed it with the aid of several trees, got to the top, and headed over more even ground in the direction the voices had come from. There was a lot of underbrush, though, and she swerved around several thorny, close-packed patches of it. At each swerve she kept her eyes pointed in the direction of the main trail. She walked in this fashion for ten minutes or so, then stopped. In that tender place between her chest and her stomach, the place where all the body's wires seemed to come together in a clump, she felt the first minnowy flutter of disquiet. Shouldn't she have come to the North Conway branch of the Appalachian Trail by now? It certainly seemed so; she hadn't gone far down the Kezar Notch branch, probably not more than fifty paces (*surely* no more than sixty, seventy at the very most), and so the gap between the two diverging arms of the Y couldn't be very big, could it?

She listened for voices on the main trail, but now the woods were silent. Well, that wasn't true. She could hear the sough of the wind through the big old west-country pines, she could hear the squawk of a jay and the far-off hammering of a woodpecker digging his midmorning snack out of a hollow tree, she could hear a couple of freshly arrived mosquitoes (they were buzzing around both ears now), but no human voices. It was as if she were the only person in all these big woods, and although that was ridiculous, the minnow fluttered in that hollow place once more. A little more strongly this time.

Trisha started walking forward again, faster now, wanting to get to the trail, wanting the relief of the trail. She came to a great fallen tree, too high to climb over, and decided to wriggle under it instead. She knew the smart thing would be to go around, but what if she lost her bearings?

You've already lost them, a voice in her head whispered – a terrible cold voice.

'Shut up, I have not, you shut up,' she whispered back, and dropped to her knees. There was a hollow running beneath one section of the moss-caked old trunk, and Trisha squirmed into it. The leaves lining it were wet, but by the time she realized this the front of her shirt was already soaked through and she decided it didn't matter. She wriggled further and her pack hit the trunk of the tree – thump.

'Damn and blast!' she whispered (*damn and blast* was her and Pepsi's current favorite swear – it sounded so English country-house, somehow) and backed up. She got to her knees, brushed clinging damp leaves from her shirt, and noticed as she did that her fingers were trembling.

'I'm not scared,' she said, speaking out loud on purpose because the sound of her voice whispering was freaking her out a little. 'Not scared a bit. The trail's right there. I'll be on it in five minutes, and running to catch up.' She took off her pack and, pushing it ahead of her, began to crawl under the tree again.

Halfway out, something moved under her. She looked down and saw a fat black snake slithering through the leaves. For a moment every thought in her mind disappeared into a silent white explosion of revulsion and horror. Her skin turned to ice and her throat closed. She could not even think the single word *snake* but only feel it, coldly pulsing under her warm hand. Trisha shrieked and tried to bolt to her feet, forgetting that she wasn't yet in the clear. A stump of branch thick as an amputated forearm poked agonizingly into the small of her back. She went flat on her stomach again and wriggled out from under the tree as fast as she could, probably looking a bit like a snake herself.

The nasty thing was gone, but her terror lingered. It had been right under her hand, hidden in the dead leaves and *right under her hand*. Evidently not a biter, thank God. But what if there were more? What if *they* were poisonous? What if the woods were full of them? And of course they were, the woods were full of everything you didn't like, everything you were afraid of and instinctively loathed, everything that tried to overwhelm you with nasty, no-brain panic. Why had she ever agreed to come? Not only agreed but agreed *cheerfully*?

She snagged the strap of her pack in one hand and hurried on with it banging against her leg, casting mistrustful looks back at the fallen tree and the leafy spaces between the standing ones, afraid of seeing the snake, even more afraid that she might see a whole battalion of them, like snakes in a horror movie, *Invasion of the Killer Snakes,* starring Patricia McFarland, the riveting tale of a little girl lost in the woods and—

'I am *not* l—' Trisha began, and then, because she was

looking back over her shoulder, she tripped on a rock sticking out of the mulchy earth, staggered, waved the arm not holding her pack in a doomed effort to keep her balance, and then fell heavily on her side. This sent up a flare of pain from her lower back, where the stump of branch had jabbed her.

She lay on her side in the leaves (damp, but not all nasty-squelchy like the ones in the hollow beneath the fallen tree), breathing fast, feeling a pulse throb between her eyes. She was suddenly, dismally aware that she didn't know if she was going in the right direction anymore or not. She had kept looking back over her shoulder, and she might not be.

Go back to the tree, then. The fallen tree. Stand where you came out from underneath and look straight ahead and that's the direction you want to go in, the direction of the main trail.

But was it? If so, how come she hadn't come to the main trail already?

Tears prickled the corners of her eyes. Trisha blinked them back savagely. If she started to cry, she wouldn't be able to tell herself she wasn't frightened. If she started to cry, anything might happen.

She walked slowly back to the fallen, moss-plated tree, hating to go in the wrong direction even for a few seconds, hating to go back to where she had seen the snake (poisonous or not, she loathed them), knowing she had to. She spotted the divot in the leaves where she'd been when she saw (and – oh God – *felt*) the snake, a girl-length smutch on the floor of the forest. It was already filling up with water. Looking at it, she rubbed a hand dispiritedly down the front of her shirt again – all damp and muddy. That her shirt should be damp and muddy from crawling under a tree was somehow the most alarming thing so far. It suggested that there had been a change of plan . . . and when the new plan included crawling through soggy hollows under fallen trees, the change was not for the better.

Why had she left the path in the first place? Why had she left *sight* of the path? Just to pee? To pee when she didn't even need to that badly? If so, she must have been crazy. And then some further craziness had possessed her, making her think she could walk through the uncharted woods (this was the phrase which occurred to her now) in safety. Well, she had learned something today, indeed she had. She had learned to stay on the path. No matter what you had to do or how bad you had to do it, no matter how much yatata-yatata you had to listen to, it was better to stay on the path. When you were on the path your Red Sox shirt stayed clean and dry. On the path there was no disturbing little minnow swimming in the hollow place between your chest and your stomach. On the path you were safe.

Safe.

Trisha reached around to the small of her back and felt a ragged hole in her shirt. The stub of branch had punched through, then. She had been hoping it hadn't. And when she brought her fingers back, there were little smears of blood on the tips. Trisha made a sighing, sobbing sound and wiped her fingers on her jeans.

'Relax, at least it wasn't a rusty nail,' she said. 'Count your blessings.' That was one of her mother's sayings, and it didn't help. Trisha had never felt less blessed in her life.

She looked along the length of the tree, even scuffed

25

one sneakered foot through the leaves, but there was no sign of the snake. It probably hadn't been one of the biting kind, anyway, but God, they were so *horrible*. All legless and slithery, flipping their nasty tongues in and out. She could hardly stand to think of it, even now – how it had pulsed under her palm like a cold muscle.

Why didn't I wear boots? Trisha thought, looking at her low-topped Reeboks. *Why am I out here in a pair of damned sneakers?* The answer, of course, was because sneakers were fine for the path . . . and the plan had been to stay on the path.

Trisha closed her eyes for a moment. 'I'm okay, though,' she said. 'All I have to do is keep my head and not go bazonka. I'll hear people over there in a minute or two, anyway.'

This time her voice convinced her a little and she felt better. She turned around, placed her feet on either side of the black divot where she had lain, and put her butt against the mossy trunk of the tree. There. Straight ahead. The main trail. Had to be.

Maybe. And maybe I better wait here. Wait for voices. Make sure I'm going the right way.

But she couldn't bear to wait. She wanted to be back on the path and putting these scary ten minutes (or maybe now it was fifteen) behind her as soon as she could. So she slipped her pack over her shoulders again – there was no angry, distracted, but basically nice big brother to check the straps for her this time – and set off again. The minges and noseeums had found her now, so many of them buzzing around her head that her vision seemed to dance with black specks. She waved at them but didn't slap. Slap at mosquitoes, but it's better just to wave at the little ones, her Mom had told her . . . perhaps on the same day she had taught Trisha how girls peed in the woods. Quilla Andersen (only then she had still been Quilla McFarland) said that slapping actually seemed to *draw* the minges and noseeums . . . and of course it made the slapper increasingly aware of her discomfort. *When it comes to bugs in the woods,* Trisha's Mom had said, *it's better to think like a horse. Pretend you've got a tail to swish em away with.*

Standing by the fallen tree, waving at the bugs but not slapping at them, Trisha had fixed her eyes on a tall pine about forty yards away . . . forty yards north, if she still had her bearings. She walked to this, and once she was standing there with her hand on the big pine's sap-tacky trunk, she looked back at the fallen tree. Straight line? She thought so.

Encouraged, she now sighted on a clump of bushes dotted with bright red berries. Her mother had pointed them out on one of their nature-walks, and when Trisha explained they were birdberries and deadly poison – Pepsi Robichaud had told her so – her mother had laughed and said, *The famous Pepsi doesn't know everything after all. That's kind of a relief. Those are checkerberries, Trish. They're not a bit poison. They taste like Teaberry gum, the kind that comes in the pink pack.* Her mother had tossed a handful of the berries into her mouth, and when she didn't fall down, choking and convulsing, Trisha had tried a few herself. To her they had tasted like gumdrops, the green ones that made your mouth feel kind of tingly.

She walked to the bushes, thought about picking a few berries just to cheer herself up, but didn't. She wasn't hungry, and had never felt less capable of cheering up. She inhaled the spicy smell of the waxy green leaves (also good to eat, Quilla had said, although Trisha had never tried them – she wasn't a woodchuck, after all), then looked back at the pine. She ascertained that she was still traveling in a straight line, and picked out a third landmark – this time a split rock that looked like a hat in an old black and white movie. Next came a cluster of birches, and from the birches she walked slowly to a luxuriant nestle of ferns halfway up a slope.

She was concentrating so fiercely on keeping each landmark in view (no more looking back over your shoulder, sweetheart) that she was standing beside the ferns before she realized she was, you should pardon the pun, overlooking the forest for the trees. Going landmark to landmark was all very well, and she thought she had managed to keep on a straight line . . . but what if it was a straight line in the wrong direction? It might be the wrong direction just by a little, but she *had* to have gone wrong. If not, she would've come to the trail again by now. Why, she must have walked . . .

'Cripes,' she said, and there was a funny little gulp in her voice that she didn't like, 'it must be a mile. A mile at *least*.'

Bugs all around her. Minges and noseeums in front of her eyes, hateful mosquitoes seeming to hang like helicopters by her ears, giving off that maddening warble-whine. She slapped at one and missed, succeeding only in making her own ear ring. And still she had to restrain herself from smacking again. If she started doing that, she'd end up whacking away at herself like a character in an old cartoon.

She dropped her pack, squatted, undid the buckles, turned back the flap. Here was her blue plastic poncho, and the paper sack with the lunch she had fixed herself; here was her Gameboy and some suntan lotion (wouldn't need that, with the sun now completely gone and the last patches of blue overhead filling in); here was her bottle of water and a bottle of Surge and her Twinkies and a bag of chips. No bug-spray, though. Wouldn't you know it. So Trisha put on the suntan lotion instead – it might keep at least the minges away – and then returned everything to her pack. She paused just a moment to look at the Twinkies, then dumped the package in with the rest. As a rule she loved them – when she got to be Pete's age her face would probably be one great big pimple if she didn't learn to lay off the sweets – but for the time being she still felt totally unhungry.

Besides, you may never get to be Pete's age, that disquieting inner voice said. How could anyone have such a cold and scary voice inside them? Such a traitor to the cause? *You may never get out of these woods.*

'Shut up, shut up, *shut up,*' she hissed, and buckled the pack's flap with trembling fingers. That done, she started to get up . . . and then paused, one knee planted in the soft earth beside the ferns, her head up, scenting the air like a fawn on its first expedition away from its mother's side. Only Trisha wasn't smelling; she was listening, focusing on that one sense with all of her concentration.

Branches rattling in a faint breath of breeze. Whining mosquitoes (rotten, nasty old things). The woodpecker. The far-off caw of a crow. And, at the furthest outpost between silence and audition, the drone of a plane. No voices from the path. Not a single voice. It was as if the trail to North

Conway had been canceled. And as the plane's motor faded away completely, Trisha conceded the truth.

She got to her feet, her legs feeling heavy, her stomach feeling heavy. Her head felt light and strange, a gas-filled balloon tethered to a lead weight. She was suddenly drowning in isolation, choking on a bright and yet oppressive sense of herself as a living being cast out from her fellows. She had somehow gotten out of bounds, wandered off the playing field and into a place where the rules she was used to no longer applied.

'*Hey!*' she screamed. '*Hey, someone, do you hear me? Do you hear me? Hey!*' She paused, praying for an answer to come back, but no answer came and so she brought the worst out at last: '*Help me, I'm lost! Help me, I'm lost!*' Now the tears began to come and she could no longer hold them back, could no longer kid herself that she was in charge of this situation. Her voice trembled, became first the wavery voice of a little kid and then almost the shriek of a baby who lies forgotten in her pram, and that sound frightened her more than anything else so far on this awful morning, the only human sound in the woods her weepy, shrieking voice calling for help, calling for help because she was lost.

THIRD INNING

She yelled for perhaps fifteen minutes, sometimes cupping her hands around her mouth and turning her voice in the direction she imagined the main trail must be, mostly just standing there by the ferns and screaming. She gave one final shriek − no words, just a high birdcall of combined anger and fear − so loud it hurt her throat, then sat down beside her pack and put her face in her hands and cried. She cried hard for maybe five minutes (it was impossible to tell for sure, her watch was back home, lying on the table next to her bed, another smooth move by the Great Trisha), and when she stopped she felt a little better . . . except for the bugs. The bugs were everywhere, crawling and whining and buzzing, trying to drink her blood and sip her sweat. The bugs were driving her crazy. Trisha got to her feet again, waving the air with her Red Sox cap, reminding herself not to slap, knowing she *would* slap, and soon, if things didn't change. She wouldn't be able to help herself.

Walk or stay where she was? She didn't know which would be best; she was now too frightened for anything much like rational thought. Her feet decided for her and Trisha got moving again, looking around fearfully as she went, wiping her swollen eyes with her arm. The second time she raised the arm to her face she saw half a dozen mosquitoes on it and slapped at them blindly, killing three. Two had been full to bursting. The sight of her own blood didn't ordinarily upset her, but this time all the strength went out of her legs and she sat down again on the needle-carpet in a cluster of old pines and cried some more. She felt headachy and a little whoopsy in her stomach. *But I was just in the van a little while ago,* she thought over and over. *Just in the van, the back seat of the van, listening to them snipe at each other.* And then she thought of her brother's angry voice drifting through the trees: — *don't know why we have to pay for what you guys did wrong!* It occurred to her that those might be the last words she would ever hear Pete say, and she actually shuddered at the idea, as at the sight of some monstrous shape in the shadows.

Her tears dried up more quickly this time and the weeping wasn't so intense. When she got to her feet again (waving her cap around her head almost without realizing it) she felt halfway to being calm. By now they'd surely know she was gone. Mom's first thought would be that Trisha had gotten pissed at them for arguing and gone back to the Caravan. They'd call out for her, then retrace their steps, asking people they met on the trail if they'd seen a girl in a Red Sox cap (*she's nine but tall for her age and looks older,* Trisha could hear her Mom saying), and when they got back to the parking area and found she wasn't in the van, they'd start getting seriously worried. Mom would be frightened. The thought of her fright made Trisha feel guilty as well as afraid. There was going to be a fuss, maybe a big one involving the game wardens and the Forest Service, and it was all her fault. She had left the path.

This added a new layer of anxiety to her already disturbed mind and Trisha began to walk fast, hoping to get back to the main trail before all those calls could be made, before she could turn into what her mother called A Public Spectacle. She walked without taking her previous, meticulous care in moving from point to point in a straight line, turning more and more to the west without realizing it, turning away from the Appalachian Trail and most of its subsidiary paths and trails, turning in a direction where there was little but deep second-growth woods choked with underbrush, tangled ravines, and ever more difficult terrain. She alternately called and listened, listened and called. She would have been stunned to learn that her mother and brother were still locked in their argument and did not know, even yet, that Trisha was missing.

She walked faster and faster, waving at the swirling clouds of minges, no longer bothering to skirt clumps of bushes but simply plowing straight through them. She listened and called, called and listened, except she *wasn't* listening, not really, not anymore. She didn't feel the mosquitoes that were clustered on the back of her neck, lined up just below her hairline like drinkers at happy hour, guzzling their fill; she didn't feel the noseeums caught and wriggling in the faint sticky lines where her tears were still drying.

Her giving way to panic wasn't sudden, as it had been at the feel of the snake, but weirdly gradual, a drawing in from the world, a shutting down of outer awareness. She walked faster without minding her way; called for help without hearing her own voice; listened with ears that might not have heard a returning shout from behind the nearest tree. And when she began to run she did it without realizing. *I have to be calm,* she thought as her sneakered feet sped past the point of jogging. *I was just in the van,* she thought as the run became a sprint. *I don't know why we should pay for what you guys did wrong,* she thought, ducking – barely – a jutting branch that seemed to thrust itself at one of her eyes. It scraped the side of her face instead, drawing a thin scrawl of blood from her left cheek.

The breeze in her face as she ran, tearing through a thicket with a crackling sound that seemed very distant (she was unaware of the thorns which ripped at her jeans and tore shallow gouges on her arms), was cool and strangely exhilarating. She pelted up a slope, now running full-out with her hat on crooked and her hair flying behind her – the rubber-band which had held it in a ponytail was long since lost – hurdling small trees which had fallen in some long-ago storm, topping a ridge . . . and suddenly there was a long blue-gray valley spread out before her with brazen granite cliffs rising on the far side, miles from where she was. And directly in front of her nothing but a gray shimmer of early summer air through which she would fall to her death, turning over and over and screaming for her mother.

Her mind was gone again, lost in that white no-brain roar of terror, but her body recognized that stopping in time to avoid going over the cliff-edge was an impossibility. All she could hope to do was redirect her motion before it was too late. Trisha swerved to the left, and as she did her right foot kicked out over the drop. She could hear the pebbles dislodged by that foot rattling down the ancient rock wall in a little stream.

Trisha bolted along the strip where the needle-coated floor of the forest gave way to the bald rock marking the edge of the cliff. She ran with some confused and roaring knowledge of what had almost happened to her, and also some vague memory of a science fiction movie in which the hero had lured a rampaging dinosaur into running over a cliff to its death.

Ahead of her an ash tree had fallen with its final twenty feet jutting over the drop like the prow of a ship, and Trisha grabbed it with both arms and hugged it, her scraped and bloody cheek jammed against the smooth trunk, each breath whistling into her with a shriek and emerging in a terrified sob. She stood that way for a long time, shuddering all over and embracing the tree. At last she opened her eyes. Her head was turned to the right and she was looking down before she could stop herself.

At this point the cliff's drop was only fifty feet, ending in a pile of glacial, splintery rubble that sprouted little clumps of bright green bushes. There was a heap of rotting trees and branches, as well − deadwood blown over the cliff's edge in some long-ago storm. An image came to Trisha then, one that was terrible in its utter clarity. She saw herself falling toward that jackstraw pile, screaming and waving her arms as she went down; saw a dead branch punching through the undershelf of her jaw and up between her teeth, tacking her tongue to the roof of her mouth like a red memo, then spearing into her brain and killing her.

'*No!*' she screamed, both revolted by the image and terrified by its plausibility. She caught her breath.

'I'm all right,' she said, speaking low and fast. The bramble-scratches on her arms and the scrape on her cheek throbbed and stung with sweat − she was just now becoming aware of these little hurts. 'I'm okay. I'm all right. Yeah, baby.' She let go of the ash tree, swayed on her feet, then clutched it again as panic lunged inside her head. An irrational part of her actually expected the ground to tilt and spill her off the edge.

'I'm okay,' she said, still low and fast. She licked her upper lip and tasted damp salt. 'I'm okay, I'm okay.' She repeated it over and over, but it was still three minutes before she could persuade her arms to loosen their death-clutch on the ash tree a second time. When she finally managed it, Trisha stepped back, away from the drop. She reset her cap (turning it around so the bill pointed backward without even thinking about it) and looked out across the valley. She saw the sky, now sagging with rainclouds, and she saw roughly six trillion trees, but she saw no sign of human life — not even smoke from a single campfire.

'I'm all right, though — I'm okay.' She took another step back from the drop and uttered a little scream as something

(*snakes snakes*)

brushed the backs of her knees. Just bushes, of course. More checkerberry bushes, the woods were full of em, yuck-yuck. And the bugs had found her again. They were re-forming their cloud, hundreds of tiny black spots dancing around her eyes, only this time the spots were bigger and seemed to be bursting open like the blooms of black roses. Trisha had just time enough to think, *I'm fainting, this is fainting,* and then she went down on her back in the bushes, her eyes rolled up to whites, the bugs hanging in a shimmering cloud above her small pallid face. After a moment or two the first mosquitoes alit on her eyelids and began to feed.

36

TOP OF THE FOURTH

Her mother was moving furniture – that was Trisha's first returning thought. Her second was that Dad had taken her to Good Skates in Lynn and what she heard was the sound of kids rollerblading past on the old canted track. Then something cold splashed onto the bridge of her nose and she opened her eyes. Another cold drop of water splashed down dead center on her forehead. Bright light ran across the sky, making her wince and squint. This was followed by a second crash of thunder that startled her into a sideways roll. She pulled instinctively into a fetal position, uttering a croaky little scream as she did so. Then the skies opened.

Trisha sat up, grabbing and replacing her baseball cap when it fell off without even thinking about it, gasping like someone who has been tossed rudely into a cold lake (and that was what it felt like). She staggered to her feet. Thunder boomed again and lightning opened a purple seam in the air. As she stood with rain dripping from the tip of her nose and her hair lying lank against her cheeks, she saw a tall, half-dead spruce on the valley floor below her suddenly explode and fall in two flaming pieces. A moment later the rain was sheeting down so thickly that the valley was only a sketched ghost wrapped in gray gauze.

She backed up, getting into the cover of the woods

again. She knelt, opened her pack, and got out the blue poncho. She put it on (*better late than never,* her father would have said) and sat on a fallen tree. Her head was still woozy and her eyelids were all swollen and itchy. The surrounding woods caught some of the rain but not all of it; the downpour was too fierce. Trisha flipped up the poncho's hood and listened to the drops tap on it, like rain on the roof of a car. She saw the ever-present cloud of bugs dancing in front of her eyes and waved at them with a strengthless hand. *Nothing makes them go away and they're always hungry, they fed on my eyelids when I was passed out and they'll feed on my dead body,* she thought, and began to cry again. This time it was low and dispirited. As she wept she continued waving at the bugs, cringing each time the thunder roared overhead.

With no watch and no sun there was no time. All Trisha knew was that she sat there, a small figure in a blue poncho huddled on a fallen tree, until the thunder began to fade eastward, sounding to her like a vanquished but still truculent bully. Rain dripped down on her. Mosquitoes hummed, one caught between the inside wall of her poncho's hood and the side of her head. She jabbed a thumb against the outside of the hood and the hum abruptly stopped.

'There,' she said disconsolately. 'That takes care of you, you're jam.' She started to get up and her stomach rumbled. She hadn't been hungry before but she was now. The thought that she had been lost long enough to get hungry was awful in its own way. She wondered how many more awful things were waiting and was glad she didn't know, couldn't see. *Maybe none,* she told herself. *Hey, girl, get happy – maybe all the awful things are behind you now.*

Trisha took off her poncho. Before opening her pack,

she looked ruefully down at herself. She was wet from head to toe and covered with pine needles from her faint – her very first fainting spell. She would have to tell Pepsi, always assuming she ever saw Pepsi again.

'Don't start that,' she said, and unbuckled the pack's flap. She took out the stuff she had brought to eat and drink, laying the items out before her in a neat line. At the sight of the paper sack with her lunch in it, her stomach rumbled more fiercely. How late *was* it? Some deep mental clock attached to her metabolism suggested it might be around three in the afternoon, eight hours since she'd sat in the breakfast nook slurping up Corn Flakes, five since she'd started off on this endless idiotic shortcut. Three o'clock. Maybe even four.

In her lunch-sack was a hardboiled egg still in the shell, a tuna fish sandwich, and some celery sticks. There was also the bag of chips (small), the bottle of water (pretty big), the bottle of Surge (the large twenty-ounce size, she loved Surge), and the Twinkies.

Looking at the bottle of lemon-lime soda, Trisha suddenly felt more thirsty than hungry . . . and mad for sugar. She spun off the cap, brought the bottle to her lips, then paused. It wouldn't be smart to go chugging half of it down, she thought, thirsty or not. She might be out here awhile. Part of her mind moaned and tried to draw away from that idea, just call it ridiculous and draw away, but Trisha couldn't afford to let it. She could think like a kid again once she was out of the woods, but for the time being she had to think as much like an adult as possible.

You saw what's out there, she thought, *a big valley with nothing in it except trees. No roads, no smoke. You have to play it smart. You have to conserve your supplies. Mom would tell you the same thing and so would Dad.*

She allowed herself three big gulps of soda, took the bottle away from her mouth, belched, took another two fast swallows. Then she recapped the bottle securely and debated over the rest of her supplies.

She decided on the egg. She shelled it, careful to put the pieces of shell back in the Baggie the egg had come in (it never occurred to her, then or later, that littering — any sign that she'd been there — might actually save her life), and sprinkled it with the little twist of salt. Doing that made her sob briefly again, because she could see herself in the Sanford kitchen last night, putting salt on a scrap of waxed paper and then twisting it up the way her mother had shown her. She could see the shadows of her head and hands, thrown by the overhead light, on the Formica counter; she could hear the sound of the TV news from the living room; could hear creaks as her brother moved around upstairs. This memory had a hallucinogenic clarity that elevated it almost to the status of a vision. She felt like someone who drowns remembering what it was like to still be on the boat, so calm and at ease, so carelessly safe.

She was nine, though, nine going on ten and big for her age. Hunger was stronger than either memory or fear. She sprinkled the egg with salt and ate it quickly, still sniffling. It was delicious. She could have eaten another easily, maybe two. Mom called eggs 'cholesterol bombs,' but her Mom wasn't here and cholesterol didn't seem like a very big deal when you were lost in the woods, scratched up and with your eyelids so swollen by bug-bites that they

40

felt weighted down with something (flour-paste stuck to the lashes, perhaps).

Trisha eyed the Twinkies, then opened the package and ate one of them. '*SECK*-shoo-al,' she said – one of Pepsi's all-time-great compliments. She chased everything with a gulp of water. Then, moving quickly before either hand could turn traitor and stuff something else into her mouth, she put the remaining food back in the lunch-sack (the top rolled down quite a bit further now), rechecked the seal on her three-quarter-full bottle of Surge, and stowed everything in the pack. As she did, her fingers brushed a bulge in the pack's sidewall and a sudden burst of elation – perhaps partially fueled by fresh calories – lit her up.

Her Walkman! She had brought her Walkman! Yeah, baby!

She unzipped the inner pocket and lifted it out as reverently as any priest has ever handled the eucharist. The headphone wire was wrapped around the body of the Walkman and the tiny earbuds were clipped neatly to the sides of its black plastic body. Her and Pepsi's current favorite tape (*Tubthumper,* by Chumbawamba) was in there, but Trisha didn't care about music just then. She slipped the headphones on, nestled the earbuds into place, flipped the switch from TAPE to RADIO, and turned it on.

At first there was nothing but a soft rush of static, because she had been tuned to WMGX, a Portland station. But a little further down the FM band she came to WOXO in Norway, and when she tuned up the other way she got WCAS, the little station in Castle Rock, a town they had passed through on their way to the Appalachian Trail. She could almost hear her brother, his voice dripping with that newly discovered teenage sarcasm of his, saying something like '*WCAS! Hicksville today, tomorrow the world!*' And it *was* a Hicksville station, no doubt about that. Whiny cowboy singers like Mark Chestnutt and Trace Adkins alternated with a female announcer who took calls from people who wanted to sell washers, dryers, Buicks, and hunting rifles. Still, it was human contact, voices in the wilderness, and Trisha sat on the fallen tree, transfixed, waving absently at the constant cloud of bugs with her cap. The first time-check she heard was three-oh-nine.

At three thirty, the female announcer put the Community Trading Post on hold long enough to read the local news. Folks in Castle Rock were up in arms about a bar where there were now topless dancers on Friday and Saturday nights, there had been a fire at a local nursing home (no one hurt), and Castle Rock Speedway was supposed to re-open on the Fourth of July with brand new stands and loads of fireworks. Rainy this afternoon, clearing tonight, sunny tomorrow with highs in the mid-eighties. That was it. No missing little girl. Trisha didn't know whether to be relieved or worried.

She reached to turn off the power and save the batteries, then paused as the female announcer added, 'Don't forget that the Boston Red Sox take on those pesky New York Yankees tonight at seven o'clock; you can catch all the action right here on WCAS, where we've got our Sox on. And now back to—'

Now back to the shittiest day a little girl ever had, Trisha thought, turning off the radio and wrapping the cord around the slim plastic body again. Yet the truth was that she felt almost all right for the first time since that nasty minnow had started swimming around in her midsection. Having something to eat was partially the reason, but she suspected that the radio had more to do with it. Voices, real human voices, and sounding so close.

There was a cluster of mosquitoes on each of her thighs, trying to drill through the material of her jeans. Thank God she hadn't worn shorts. She would have been chuck steak by now.

She swatted the mosquitoes away, then got up. What now? Did she know anything at all about being lost in the woods? Well, that the sun rose in the east and went down in the west; that was about all. Once someone had told her that moss grew on the north or south side of a tree, but she couldn't remember which. Maybe the best thing would be just to sit here, try to make some sort of shelter (more against the bugs than the rain, there were mosquitoes inside the hood of her poncho again and they were driving her crazy), and wait for someone to come. If she had matches, maybe she could make a fire – the rain would keep it from spreading – and someone would see the smoke. Of course, if pigs had wings, bacon would fly. Her father said that.

'Wait a minute,' she said. 'Wait a minute.'

Something about water. Finding your way out of the woods by water. Now what – ?

It came to her, and she felt another burst of elation. This one was so strong that it made her feel almost giddy; she actually swayed a little on her feet, as one will at the sound of catchy music.

You found a stream. Her mother hadn't told her that, she had read it in one of the *Little House* books a long time ago, maybe way back when she'd been seven. You found a stream and followed it and sooner or later it would either lead you out or to a bigger stream. If it was a bigger stream, you followed it until it led you out or to a bigger stream yet. But in the end running water *had* to lead you out because it always ran to the sea, and there were no woods there, only the beach and rocks and the occasional lighthouse. And how would she find running water? Why, she would follow the bluff, of course. The one she had almost run off the edge of, stupidnik that she was. The bluff would lead her in one steady direction, and sooner or later she'd find a brook. The woods were full of em, as the saying went.

She reshouldered her pack (this time putting it on over the poncho) and walked carefully toward the bluff and the fallen ash tree. She now looked back on her panicky plunge through the woods with the mixture of indulgence and embarrassment adults feel when looking back upon the worst of their childhood behavior, but she found she could still not go very close to the edge. It would make her feel sick if she did. She might faint again . . . or vomit. Vomiting up any of her food when she had so little would be a very bad idea.

She turned to the left and began walking through the woods with the drop-off to the valley about twenty feet to her right. Every now and then she would force herself to go closer and make sure she wasn't drifting away — that the bluff with its wide view was still there. She listened for voices, but not very hopefully; the trail might be anywhere now, and to stumble on it would be pure dumb luck. What she was listening for was running water, and at last she heard it.

Won't do me any good if it goes over that stupid cliff in a waterfall, she thought, and decided she had to get close enough to the edge to check out the drop before she reached the stream. If only to guard against disappointment.

The trees had drawn back a little here, and the space between the edge of the forest and the edge of the drop was dotted with bushes. They would, four or five weeks later, bear a lush crop of blueberries. Now, however, the berries were just tiny buds, green and inedible. Still, there had been checkerberries; *they* were in season, and it might be a good idea to keep that in mind. Just in case.

The ground between the blueberry bushes was scaly and shifty with busted rock. The sound under Trisha's sneakers made her think of broken plates. She walked ever more slowly over this scree, and when she was ten feet or so from the edge of the drop, she got down and crawled. *I'm safe, perfectly safe because I know it's there, nothing to worry about,* but her heart was still hammering in her chest. And when she got to the edge she uttered a bewildered little laugh because the drop was hardly there at all anymore.

The view across the valley was still wide and sweeping but wouldn't be for much longer, because the terrain on this side had been sinking – Trisha had been listening so hard and thinking so hard (mostly reminding herself to keep her head, not to go bazonka again) that she hadn't even realized. She worked her way further, pushing through a final little screen of bushes, and looked down.

The drop was now only about twenty feet, and no longer sheer – the rock face had become a steep, rubbly slope. Down below were scrubby trees, more fruitless blueberry bushes, tangles of brambles. And scattered everywhere were heaps of broken-up glacial rock. The downpour had stopped, the thunder had retreated to the occasional ill-natured mutter, but it had continued to drizzle and these heaps of rock had a slick, unpleasant look, like slag from a mine.

Trisha backed up and got to her feet, then continued to make her way through the bushes toward the sound of running water. She was starting to feel tired now, her legs aching, but she thought she was basically okay. Afraid, of course, but not so badly as before. They would find her. When people got lost in the woods they always found them. They sent out planes and helicopters and guys with bloodhounds and they hunted until the lost person was found.

Or maybe I'll kind of save myself. Find a camp in the woods somewhere, break a window if the door's locked and there's no one home, use the telephone . . .

Trisha could see herself in some hunter's cabin which hadn't been used since the previous fall; she could see camp furniture covered with faded paisley dropcloths and a bearskin rug on the board floor. She could smell dust and old stove ashes; this daydream was so clear she could even smell a trace of ancient coffee. The place was empty but the telephone worked. It was one of the oldfashioned ones, the handset so heavy that she had to hold it in both hands, but it worked and she could hear herself saying: 'Hello, Mom? This is Trisha. I don't know exactly where I am, but I'm all r—'

She was so absorbed in the imaginary cabin and the imaginary phone call that she came close to falling into a small stream that emerged from the woods and cascaded down the rubble-strewn slope.

Trisha grabbed at the branches of an alder and stood looking at the stream, actually smiling a little. It had been a crappy day, all right, *très* crappy, but her luck finally seemed to be turning and that was a big hooray. She walked to the edge of the slope. The stream spilled down it in a foamy rush, here and there striking a bigger rock and kicking up spray that would have held rainbows on a sunny afternoon. The slope on both sides of the water looked slippery and unreliable – all that loose wet rock. Still, it was also dotted with bushes. If she started to slide, she would grab one of those as she'd grabbed the alder at the edge of the stream.

'Water leads to people,' she said, and started down the slope.

She descended sideways, in little hops, on the right side of the stream. At first she was all right even though the angle of the slope was steeper than it had looked from up above and the broken ground shifted under her sneakers every time she moved. Her pack, of which she had hardly been aware up until now, began to feel like a large, unstable baby in one of those papoose carriers; every time it shifted she had to wave her arms to keep her balance. She was all right, though, and a darn good thing, because when she paused halfway down the slope, her propping right foot actually buried in loose rock below her, she realized she couldn't climb back up anymore. One way or the other, she was bound for the valley floor.

She got moving again. Three quarters of the way down, a bug – a big one, not a minge or a mosquito – flew into her face. It was a wasp, and Trisha batted at it with a cry. Her pack shifted violently to her downhill side, her right foot slipped, and suddenly her balance was gone. She fell, hit the rock slope on her shoulder with a tooth-rattling thud, and began to slide.

'*Oh shit on toast!*' she cried, and grabbed at the ground. All she got was a strew of loose rock that slid along with her and a sharp jab of pain as a broken chunk of quartz cut her palm. She snatched at a bush and it came out by its stupid shallow roots. Her foot struck something, her right leg bent at a painful angle, and she was suddenly airborne, the world revolving as she did an unplanned somersault.

Trisha came down on her back and slid that way, legs spread, arms waving, screaming in pain and terror and surprise. Her poncho and the back of her shirt pulled up to her shoulderblades; sharp pieces of rock tore snatches of skin from between them. She tried to brake with her feet. The left one struck a jutting outcrop of shale and turned her to the right. That put her into a roll – first on her stomach and then onto her back and then onto her stomach again, the pack digging into her, then pitching upward each time she went over. The sky was down, the hateful broken scree of the slope was up, and then they swapped places – swing your partner with a dosey-do, everybody change.

Trisha went the final ten yards on her left side with her left arm stretched out and her face buried against the fold of her elbow. She thumped against something hard enough to bruise her ribs on that side . . . and then, before she could even look up from her arm, a needle of pain drove into her just above her left cheekbone. Trisha shrieked and jerked to her knees, slapping. She crushed something – another wasp, of course, what else – even as it stung her again, even as she opened her eyes and saw them all around her: yellow-brown insects that looked weighted down in the tailsection, plump ungainly poison factories.

She had slid into a dead tree standing at the foot of the slope about twenty-five feet from the brawling streamlet. In the dead tree's lowest fork, just at eye-level to a little girl who was nine but tall for her age, was a gray paper nest. Agitated wasps were crawling all over it; more were flying out of a hole in the top.

Pain needled the right side of Trisha's neck, just below the bill of her cap. Another sting lit up her right arm above the elbow. Screaming, in a total panic, she bolted. Something stung the back of her neck; something stung the small of her back, above the waistband of her bluejeans, where her shirt was still pulled up and the plastic poncho hung in tatters.

She ran in the direction of the stream without any thought or plan or intent; it was just that the ground there was relatively open. She wove her way around the clumps of bushes, and when the underbrush began to thicken she bulled through it. At the stream she stopped, gasping for breath, looking tearfully (and fearfully) back over her shoulder. The wasps were gone, but they had done plenty of damage before she had managed to outrun them. Her left eye, close to where the first one had gotten her, was swelled almost shut.

If I get a bad reaction, I'll die, she thought, but in the aftermath of her panic she didn't care. She sat down by the little stream which had gotten her into all this trouble, sobbing and sniffling. When she felt a little bit in control of herself again, she took off her pack. Tight, fierce shudders wracked her, each one making her body harden up like a spring and pulling red-hot darts of pain from the places where she had been stung. She put her arms around her pack, rocked it like a doll, and cried harder. Holding the pack that way made her think of Mona lying in the back seat of the Caravan, good old Moanie Balogna with her big blue eyes. There had been times, while her parents were getting ready to divorce and then actually doing it, when Mona had felt like her only comfort; there were times when not even Pepsi could understand. Now her parents' divorce seemed like very small beans. There were bigger problems than grownups who couldn't get along, there were wasps, for one thing, and Trisha thought she would give anything to see Mona again.

At least she wasn't going to die from the stings, or she'd probably be dying already. She had overheard her Mom and Mrs. Thomas from across the street talking about someone who was allergic to stings, and Mrs. Thomas had said, 'Ten seconds after it gut im, poor ole Frank was swole up like a balloon. If he hadn't had his little kit with the hyperdermic, I guess he woulda choked to death.'

Trisha didn't feel choky, but the bites throbbed horribly, and they had swole up like balloons, all right. The one by her eye had built a hot little volcano of tissue that she could actually look at, and when she probed gingerly with her fingers, a bolt of pain shot into her head and made her cry out in misery. She was no longer exactly weeping, but that eye ran helplessly with tears just the same.

Moving her hands slowly and carefully, Trisha examined herself. She isolated at least half a dozen stings (she thought there was one location, on her left side just above the hip, where she might have sustained two or even three – it was the sorest place of all). Her back felt all scraped up and her left arm, which had absorbed most of the damage during the final part of her slide, was a net of blood from wrist to elbow. The side of her face where the stump of branch had poked her was bleeding again, too.

Not fair, she thought. *Not f—*

Then a terrible idea occurred to her . . . except it was more than an idea, it was a certainty. Her Walkman was broken, shattered to a million pieces in its little side pocket. Had to be. There was no way it could have survived the slide.

Trisha tugged the pack's buckles with bloodstreaked trembling fingers and at last worked the straps free. She pulled out her Gameboy and *that* was smashed, all right, nothing left of the window where the little electronic blips had gamboled but a few shards of yellow glass. Also, her bag of potato chips had burst open and the Gameboy's cracked white housing was covered with greasy crumbs.

Both plastic bottles, the one with the water in it and the bottle of Surge, were dented but whole. Her lunchsack was smooshed into something that looked like roadkill (and covered with more potato chips), but Trisha didn't even bother looking inside. *My Walkman,* she thought, unaware that she was sobbing as she unzipped the inner pocket. *My poor poor Walkman.* To be separated from even the voices of the human world seemed more than she could bear on top of everything else.

Trisha reached into the pocket and pulled out a miracle: the Walkman, intact. The earphone cord, which she had rewrapped neatly around the little gadget's body, had come loose in a tangle, but that was all. She held the Walkman in her hand, looking incredulously from it to the Gameboy lying beside her. How could one be whole and the other so badly shattered? How was that possible?

It's not, the cold and hateful voice in her head informed her. *It* looks *all right but it's broken inside.*

Trisha straightened the cord, slipped the earbuds into place, and settled her finger on the power button. She had forgotten the stings, the insect bites, the cuts and scrapes. She closed her swollen, heavy eyelids, making a little dark. 'Please, God,' she said into it, 'don't let my Walkman be broken.' Then she pushed the power button.

'This just in,' said the female announcer – she might have been broadcasting from the middle of Trisha's head. 'A Sanford woman hiking a Castle County section of the Appalachian Trail with her two children has reported her daughter, nine-year-old Patricia McFarland, missing and presumably lost in the woods west of TR-90 and the town of Motton.'

Trisha's eyes flew wide open and she listened for the next ten minutes, long after WCAS had reverted, like someone with unbreakable bad habits, to country music and NASCAR reports. She was lost in the woods. It was official. Soon they would swing into action, whoever *they* were – the people, she supposed, who kept the helicopters ready to fly and the bloodhounds ready to sniff. Her mother would be scared to death . . . and yet Trisha felt a small strange trickle of satisfaction when she considered that likelihood.

I wasn't supervised, she thought – not without self-righteousness. *I'm just a little kid and I wasn't properly supervised. Also if she gives me hell I'll just say 'You wouldn't stop arguing and finally I couldn't stand it anymore.'* Pepsi would like that; it was just so V. C. Andrews.

At last she turned the Walkman off, rewrapped the headphone wire, gave the black plastic case a perfectly unselfconscious smooch, and tucked it lovingly back into its pocket. She eyed the mashed-up lunchbag and decided she couldn't bring herself to look inside and see what shape the tuna sandwich and the remaining Twinkie might be in. Too depressing. A good thing she'd eaten her egg before it could turn into egg salad. That thought probably deserved a giggle, but there were apparently no giggles in her; the old giggle-well, which her mother believed inexhaustible, seemed to have temporarily gone dry.

Trisha sat on the bank of the little stream, which was less than three feet across here, and disconsolately ate potato chips, first out of the burst chip-bag and then plucking them off her lunch-sack and finally dredging the smallest fragments out of the bottom of her pack. A big bug droned past her nose and she cringed from it, crying out and raising a hand to protect her face, but it was only a horsefly.

At last, moving as wearily as a woman of sixty after a hard day's work (she *felt* like a woman of sixty after a hard day's work), Trisha replaced everything in her pack – even the shattered Gameboy went back in – and stood up. Before rebuckling the flap, she took off her poncho and held it up in front of her. The flimsy thing hadn't been any protection in her slide down the slope, and now it was torn and flapping in a way she would have considered comic under other circumstances – it looked almost like a blue plastic hula skirt – but she supposed she'd better keep it. If nothing else, it might protect her from the bugs, which had reformed their cloud around her hapless head. The mosquitoes were thicker than ever, no doubt drawn by the blood on her arms. They probably smelled it.

'Yug,' Trisha said, wrinkling her nose and waving her cap at the cloud of bugs, 'how gross is that?' She tried to tell herself she ought to be grateful she hadn't broken her arm or fractured her skull, also grateful that she wasn't allergic to stings like Mrs. Thomas's friend Frank, but it was hard to be grateful when you were scared, scratched, swollen, and generally banged up.

She was putting the rags of her poncho back on – the pack would come next – when she looked at the stream and noticed how muddy the banks were just above the water. She dropped to one knee, wincing as the waist of her jeans chafed against the wasp-stings above her hip, and took up a fingerful of pasty brown-gray gluck. Try it or not?

'Well, what can it hurt?' she asked with a little sigh, and dabbed the mud on the swelling above her hip. It was blessedly cool, and the itchy pain diminished almost at once. Working carefully, she dabbed mud on as many of the stings as she could reach, including the one which had puffed up beside her eye. Then she wiped her hands on her jeans (both hands and jeans considerably more battered now than they had been six hours ago), donned her torn poncho, then shrugged into her pack. Luckily, it lay without rubbing against any of the places where she'd been stung. Trisha began walking beside the stream again, and five minutes later she re-entered the woods.

She followed the stream for the next four hours or so, hearing nothing but twitting birds and the ceaseless drone of bugs. It drizzled for most of that time, and once it showered hard enough to wet her through again even though she took shelter under the biggest tree she could find. At least there was no thunder and lightning with the second downpour.

Trisha had never felt as much like a town girl as she did while that miserable, terrifying day was winding down toward dark. The woods came in clenches, it seemed to her. For awhile she would walk through great old stands of pine, and there the forest seemed almost all right, like the woods in a Disney cartoon. Then one of those clenches would come and she would find herself struggling through snarly clumps of scrubby trees and thick bushes (all too many of the latter the kind with thorns), fighting past interlaced branches that clawed for her arms and eyes. Their only purpose seemed to be obstruction, and as mere tiredness slipped toward exhaustion, Trisha began to impute them with actual intelligence, a sly and hurtful awareness of the outsider in the ragged blue poncho. It began to seem to her that their desire to scratch her – to perhaps even get lucky and poke out one of her eyes – was actually secondary; what the bushes really wanted was to shunt her away from the brook, her path to other people, her ticket out.

Trisha was willing to leave sight of the brook if the clenches of trees and tangles of bushes near it got too thick, but she refused to leave the sound of it. If the brook's low babble got too thin, she'd drop to her hands and knees and crawl under the worst of the branches rather than sliding along them and looking for a hole. Crawling over the squelchy ground was the worst part (in the pine groves the ground was dry and nicely carpeted with needles; in the clenchy tangles it always seemed wet). Her pack dragged through the lacings of branches and bushes, sometimes actually getting stuck . . . and all the time, no matter how thick the going, the cloud of minges and noseeums hung and danced in front of her face.

She understood what made all of this so bad, so dispiriting, but could not articulate it. It had something to do with all the things she couldn't name. Some stuff she knew because her mother had told her: the birches, the beeches, the alders, the spruces and pines; the hollow hammering of a woodpecker and the harsh cawing cry of the crows; the creaky-door sound of the crickets as the day began to darken . . . but what was everything else? If her mother had told her, Trisha no longer remembered, but she didn't think her mother had told her in the first place. She thought her mother was really just a town girl from Massachusetts who had lived in Maine for awhile, liked to walk in the woods, and had read a few nature guides. What, for instance, were the thick bushes with the shiny green leaves (please God, not poison oak)? Or the small, trashy-looking trees with the dusty-gray trunks? Or the ones with the narrow hanging leaves? The woods around Sanford, the woods her mother knew and walked – sometimes with Trisha and sometimes alone – were toy woods. These were not toy woods.

Trisha tried to imagine hundreds of searchers flooding toward her. Her imagination was good, and at first she was able to do this quite easily. She saw big yellow schoolbuses with the words CHARTER SEARCH PARTY in the destination windows pulling into parking areas all along the western

Maine part of the Appalachian Trail. The doors opened and out spilled men in brown uniforms, some with dogs on chains, all with walkie-talkies clipped to their belts, a special few with those battery-powered loudhailers; these would be what she heard first, big amplified God-voices calling 'PATRICIA McFARLAND, WHERE ARE YOU? IF YOU HEAR, COME TO THE SOUND OF MY VOICE!'

But as the shadows in the woods thickened and joined hands, there was only the sound of the stream – no wider and no smaller than when she had tumbled down the slope beside it – and the sound of her own breathing. Her mental pictures of the men in the brown uniforms weakened, little by little.

I can't stay out here all night, she thought, *no one can expect me to stay out here all* night—

She felt panic trying to grab her again – it was speeding her heartbeat, drying out her mouth, making her eyes throb in their sockets. She was lost in the woods, hemmed in by trees for which she had no name, alone in a place where her town-girl vocabulary had little use, and she was consequently left with just a narrow range of recognition and reaction, all of it primitive. From town girl to cave girl in one easy step.

She was afraid of the dark even when she was at home in her room, with the glow from the streetlight on the corner falling in through the window. She thought that if she had to spend the night out here, she would die of terror.

Part of her wanted to run. Never mind how flowing water was bound to take her to people eventually, all that was likely just a crock of *Little House on the Prairie* shit.

She had been following this stream for miles now, and all it had brought her to was more bugs. She wanted to run away from it, run in whatever direction the going was easiest. Run and find people before it got dark. That the idea was totally nutso didn't help much. It certainly didn't change the throb in her eyes (and the stung places, now *they* were throbbing, too) or ease the coppery fear-taste in her mouth.

Trisha fought her way through a tangle of trees growing so close together they were almost intertwined and came out in a little crescent of clearing where the brook took an elbow-bend to the left. This crescent, hemmed in on all sides by bushes and raggedy clumps of trees, looked like a little patch of Eden to Trisha. There was even a fallen tree-trunk for a bench.

She went to it, sat down, closed her eyes, and tried to pray for rescue. Asking God to not let her Walkman be broken had been easy because it had been unthinking. Now, however, praying was hard. Neither of her parents were churchgoers – her Mom was a lapsed Catholic, and her Dad, so far as Trisha knew, had never had anything to lapse from – and now she discovered herself lost and without vocabulary in another way. She said the Our Father and it came out of her mouth sounding flat and uncomforting, about as useful as an electric can-opener would have been out here. She opened her eyes and looked around the little clearing, seeing all too well how gray the air was becoming, clasping her scratched hands nervously together.

She couldn't remember ever discussing spiritual matters with her mother, but she had asked her father not a month ago if he believed in God. They had been out behind his little place in Malden, eating ice cream cones from the Sunny Treat man, who still came by in his tinkling white truck (thinking of the Sunny Treat truck now made Trisha feel like crying again). Pete had been 'down the park,' as they said in Malden, goofing with his old friends.

'God,' Dad had said, seeming to taste the word like some new ice cream flavor – Vanilla with God instead of Vanilla with Jimmies. 'What brought that on, sugar?'

She shook her head, not knowing. Now, sitting on the fallen trunk in this cloudy, buggy June dusk, a frightening idea bloomed: what if she had asked because some deep future-seeing part of her had known that this was going to happen? Had known, had decided she was going to need a little God to get through, and had sent up a flare?

'God,' Larry McFarland had said, licking his ice cream. 'God, now, God . . .' He thought awhile longer. Trisha had sat quietly on her side of the picnic table, looking out at his little yard (it needed mowing), giving him all the time he needed. At last he said, 'I'll tell you what I believe in. I believe in the Subaudible.'

'The *what*?' She had looked at him, not sure if he was joking or not. He didn't *look* as if he was joking.

'The Subaudible. Do you remember when we lived on Fore Street?'

Of course she remembered the house on Fore Street. Three blocks from where they were, near the Lynn town line. A bigger house than this, with a bigger back yard that Dad had always kept mown. Back when Sanford was just for grandparents and summer vacations and Pepsi Robichaud was just her summer friend and arm-farts were the funniest things in the universe . . . except, of course, for real farts. On Fore Street the kitchen didn't smell of stale beer the way this house's kitchen did. She nodded, remembering very well.

'It had electric heat, that house. Do you remember how the baseboard units would hum, even when they weren't heating? Even in the summer?'

Trisha had shaken her head. And her father had nodded his, as if that was what he expected.

'That's because you got used to it,' he said. 'But take my word, Trish, that sound was always there. Even in a house where there aren't baseboard heaters, there are noises. The fridge goes on and off. The pipes thunk. The floors creak. The traffic goes by outside. We hear those things all the time, so most of the time we don't hear them at all. They become . . .' And he gestured for her to finish, as he had done since she was very small, sitting on his lap and beginning to read. His old dear gesture.

'Subaudible,' she said, not because she completely understood what the word meant but because it was so clearly what he wanted from her.

'Pree-cisely,' he said, gesturing once more with his ice cream. A splatter of vanilla drops ran up one leg of his khaki pants, and she'd found herself wondering how many beers he'd had already that day. 'Pree-cisely, sugar, subaudible. I don't believe in any actual thinking God that marks the fall of every bird in Australia or every bug in India, a God that records all of our sins in a big golden book and judges us when we die – I don't want to believe in a God who would deliberately create bad people and then deliberately send them to roast in a hell He created – but I believe there has to be *something*.'

He had looked around the yard with its too-high, too-patchy grass, the little swing-'n-gym set he had set up for his son and daughter (Pete had outgrown it, and Trisha really had, too, although she still swung or would go down the slide a few times when she was here, just to please him), the two lawn-dwarves (one barely visible in an extravagant splurge of spring weeds), the fence at the very rear that needed painting. In that moment he had looked old to her. A little confused. A little frightened. (*A little lost in the woods,* she thought now, sitting on the fallen log with her pack between her sneakers.) Then he had nodded and looked back at her.

'Yeah, something. Some kind of insensate force for the good. Insensate, do you know what that means?'

She had nodded, not knowing exactly but not wanting him to stop and explain. She didn't want him to teach her, not today; today she only wanted to learn from him.

'I think there's a force that keeps drunken teenagers – *most* drunken teenagers – from crashing their cars when they're coming home from the senior prom or their first big rock concert. That keeps most planes from crashing even when something goes wrong. Not all, just most. Hey, the fact that no one's used a nuclear weapon on actual living people since 1945 suggests there has to be *something* on our side. Sooner or later someone will, of course, but over half a century . . . that's a long time.'

He had paused, looking out at the lawn-dwarves with their vacant, cheery faces.

'There's something that keeps most of us from dying in our sleep. No perfect loving all-seeing God, I don't think the evidence supports that, but a force.'

'The Subaudible.'

'You got it.'

She had gotten it but hadn't liked it. It was too much like getting a letter you thought would be interesting and important, only when you opened it it was addressed to Dear Occupant.

'Do you believe in anything else, Dad?'

'Oh, the usual. Death and taxes and that you're the most beautiful girl in the world.'

'*Da-ad*.' She'd laughed and wriggled as he hugged her and kissed the top of her head, liking his touch and his kiss but not the smell of beer on his breath.

He let her go and stood up. 'I also believe it's beer o'clock. You want some iced tea?'

'No, thanks,' she said, and perhaps something prescient *had* been at work, because as he started away she said: '*Do* you believe in anything else? Seriously.'

His smile had faded into a look of seriousness. He stood there thinking (sitting on the log she remembered being flattered that he would think so hard on her behalf), his ice cream starting to drip over his hand now. Then he had looked up, smiling again. 'I believe that your heartthrob Tom Gordon can save forty games this year,' he said. 'I believe that right now he's the best closer in the major leagues – that if he stays healthy and the Sox hitting holds up, he could be pitching in the World Series come October. Is that enough for you?'

'*Yessss!*' she had cried, laughing, her own seriousness broken . . . because Tom Gordon really *was* her heartthrob, and she loved her father for knowing it and for being sweet about it instead of mean. She had run to him and hugged him hard, getting ice cream on her shirt and not caring. What was a little Sunny Treat between friends?

And now, sitting here in the growing grayness, listening to the drip of water all around her in the woods, watching the trees blur into shapes which would soon become threatening, listening for amplified shouts ('COME TO THE SOUND OF MY VOICE!') or the distant barking of dogs, she thought: *I can't pray to the Subaudible. I just can't.* She couldn't pray to Tom Gordon, either – that would be ludicrous – but perhaps she could listen to him pitch . . . and against the Yankees, at that. WCAS had their Sox on; she could put hers on, too. She had to conserve her batteries, she knew that, but she could listen for awhile, couldn't she? And who could tell? She might hear those amplified voices and barking dogs before the game was over.

Trisha opened her pack, reverently removed her Walkman from its inner pocket, and settled the earbuds into place. She hesitated a moment, suddenly sure the radio would no longer work, that some vital wire had been joggled loose in her tumble down the slope and this time there would be only silence when she pushed the power button. It was a stupid idea, maybe, but on a day when so many things had gone wrong, it seemed like a horribly *plausible* idea, too.

Go on, go on, don't be a chickenguts!

She pushed the button and like a miracle her head filled with the sound of Jerry Trupiano's voice . . . and more importantly, with the sounds of Fenway Park. She was sitting out here in the darkening, drippy woods, lost and alone, but she could hear thirty thousand people. It was a miracle.

63

'– comes to the belt,' Troop was saying. '*He* winds. *He* fires. And . . . *strike three called,* Martinez caught him looking! Oh, that was the slider and it was a beaut! That caught the inside corner and Bernie Williams was just frozen! Oh my! And at the end of two and a half innings, it's still the Yankees two, the Boston Red Sox nothing.'

A singing voice instructed Trisha to call 1-800-54-GIANT for some sort of auto repair, but she didn't hear it. Two and a half innings already played, which meant it had to be eight o'clock. At first that seemed amazing, and yet, given the faded quality of the light, not so hard to believe, either. She'd been on her own for ten hours. It seemed like forever; it also seemed like no time at all.

Trisha waved at the bugs (this gesture was now so automatic she didn't even realize she was doing it) and then delved into her lunchbag. The tuna sandwich wasn't as bad as she had feared, flattened and torn into hunks but still recognizably a sandwich. The Baggie had sort of kept it together. The remaining Twinkie, however, had turned into what Pepsi Robichaud would likely have called 'total sploosh.'

Trisha sat listening to the game and slowly ate half of her tuna sandwich. It awoke her appetite and she easily could have gobbled the rest, but she put it back in the bag and ate the splooshed Twinkie instead, scooping up the moist cake and the nasty-tasty white creme filling (that stuff was always creme and never cream, Trisha mused) with one finger. When she had gotten all she could with her finger, she turned the paper inside out and licked it clean. *Just call me Mrs. Sprat,* she thought, and put the Twinkie wrapper back into her lunchbag. She allowed herself three more big swallows of Surge, then went prospecting for more potato chip crumbs with the tip of one grimy finger as the Red Sox and Yankees played through the rest of the third and the fourth.

By the middle of the fifth it was four to one Yankees, with Martinez gone in favor of Jim Corsi. Larry McFarland regarded Corsi with deep mistrust. Once, while talking baseball with Trisha over the telephone, he had said: 'You mark my words, sugar – Jim Corsi is no friend of the Red Sox.' Trisha got giggling, she couldn't help it. He just sounded so *solemn*. And after awhile Dad had gotten giggling, too. It had become a catch-phrase between them, something that was just theirs, like a password: 'Mark my words, Jim Corsi is no friend of the Red Sox.'

Corsi was a friend of the Red Sox in the top of the sixth, though, getting the Yankees one-two-three. Trisha knew she should turn off the radio and conserve the batteries, Tom Gordon wasn't going to pitch in a game where the Red Sox were three runs behind, but she couldn't bear the thought of disconnecting Fenway Park. She listened to the seashell-murmur of the voices even more eagerly than to the play-by-play guys, Jerry Trupiano and Joe Castiglione. Those people were there, actually *there,* eating hotdogs and drinking beer and lining up to buy souvenirs and sof-serve ice cream and chowder from the Legal Seafood stand; they were watching as Darren Lewis – DeeLu, the announcers sometimes called him – stepped into the batter's box, the bright banks of lights casting his shadow behind him as daytime gave up overhead. She could not bear to exchange those thirty thousand murmuring voices for the low hum of mosquitoes (thicker than ever as dusk advanced), the drip of rainwater from the leaves, the rusty *rick-rick* of the crickets . . . and what other sounds there might be.

It was the other sounds she was most afraid of.

Other sounds in the dark.

DeeLu singled to right, and one out later Mo Vaughn got hold of a slider that did not slide. '*Back back WAYYY BACK!*' Troop chanted. '*That's in the Red Sox pen!* Someone – I think it might have been Rich Garces – caught it on the fly. *Home run, Mo Vaughn!* That's his twelfth of the year and the Yankee lead is cut to one.'

Sitting on her tree-trunk, Trisha laughed and clapped her hands and then resettled her signed Tom Gordon hat more firmly on her head. It was full dark now.

In the bottom of the eighth, Nomar Garciaparra hit a two-run shot into the screen on top of the Green Monster. The Red Sox took a five-to-four lead and Tom Gordon came on to pitch the top of the ninth.

Trisha slid off the fallen tree to the ground. The bark scraped against the wasp-stings on her hip, but she hardly noticed. Mosquitoes settled with immediate hungry intent on her bare back where her shirt and the tatters of the blue poncho had rucked up, but she didn't feel them. She gazed at the last held glimmerglow in the brook – fading tarnished quicksilver – and sat on the damp ground with her fingers pressed to the sides of her mouth. Suddenly it seemed very important that Tom Gordon should preserve the one-run lead, that he should secure this victory against the mighty Yankees, who had lost a pair to Anaheim at the start of the season and had hardly lost since.

'Come on, Tom,' she whispered. In a Castle View hotel room her mother was in an agony of terror; her father was on a Delta flight from Boston to Portland to join Quilla and his son; at the Castle County state police barracks, which had been designated Rally Point Patricia, search-parties very much like the ones the lost girl had imagined were coming back in after their first fruitless sallies; outside the barracks, newsvans from three TV stations in Portland and two in Portsmouth were parked; three dozen experienced woodsmen (and some *were* accompanied by dogs) remained in the forests of Motton and the three unincorporated townships which stretched off toward New Hampshire's chimney: TR-90, TR-100, and TR-110. The consensus among those remaining in the woods was that Patricia McFarland must still be in Motton or TR-90. She was a little girl, after all, and likely hadn't wandered far from where she had last been seen. These experienced guides, game wardens, and Forest Service men would have been stunned to know that Trisha had gotten almost nine miles west of the area the searchers considered their highest priority.

'Come on, Tom,' she whispered. 'Come on, Tom, one two three, now. You know how it goes.'

But not tonight. Gordon opened the top of the ninth by walking the handsome yet evil Yankee shortstop, Derek Jeter, and Trisha remembered something her father had once told her: when a team gets a lead-off walk, their chances of scoring rise by seventy percent.

If we win, if Tom gets the save, I'll be saved. This thought came to her suddenly – it was like a firework bursting in her head.

It was stupid, of course, as dopey as her father knocking on wood before a three-and-two pitch (which he did every time), but as the dark drew deeper and the brook gave up its final silver tarnish, it also seemed irrefutable, as obvious as two-and-two-makes-four: if Tom Gordon got the save, *she* would get the save.

Paul O'Neill popped up. One out. Bernie Williams came up. 'Always a dangerous hitter,' Joe Castiglione remarked, and Williams immediately ripped a single to center, sending Jeter to third.

'*Why* did you say that, Joe?' Trisha moaned. 'Oh cripes, why did you have to *say* that?'

Runners on first and third, only one out. The Fenway crowd cheering, hoping. Trisha could imagine them leaning forward in their seats.

'Come on, Tom, come *on,* Tom,' she whispered. The cloud of minges and noseeums were still all around her, but she no longer noticed. A feeling of despair touched her heart, cool and strong – it was like that hateful voice she had discovered in the middle of her head. The Yankees were too good. A base hit would tie it, a long ball would put it out of reach, and the awful, *awful* Tino Martinez was up, with the most dangerous hitter of all right behind him; the Straw Man would now be down on one knee in the on-deck circle, swinging a bat and watching.

Gordon worked the count on Martinez to two and two, then threw his curveball. '*Struck him out!*' Joe Castiglione shouted. It was as if he couldn't believe it. 'Aw, man, that was a beauty! Martinez must have missed it by a foot!'

'*Two* feet,' Troop added helpfully.

'So it all comes to this,' Joe said, and behind his voice Trisha could hear the volume of the other voices, the fan voices, begin to rise. The rhythmic clapping started. The

Fenway Faithful were getting to their feet like a church congregation about to sing a hymn. 'Two on, two out, Red Sox clinging to a one-run lead, Tom Gordon on the mound, and—'

'Don't you say it,' Trisha whispered, her hands still pressing against the sides of her mouth, 'don't you *dare* say it!'

But he did. 'And the always dangerous Darryl Strawberry coming to the plate.'

That was it; game over; great Satan Joe Castiglione had opened his mouth and jinxed it. Why couldn't he just have given Strawberry's *name*? Why did he have to start in with that 'always dangerous' horsepucky when any fool knew that only *made* them dangerous?

'All right, everybody, fasten your seatbelts,' Joe said. 'Strawberry cocks the bat. Jeter's dancing around third, trying to draw a throw or at least some attention from Gordon. He gets neither. Gordon looks in. Veritek flashes the sign. To the set. Gordon throws . . . *Strawberry swings and misses,* strike one. Strawberry shakes his head as if he's disgusted . . .'

'Shouldn't be disgusted, that was a pretty good pitch,' Troop remarked, and Trisha, sitting in the dark bugblown armpit of nowhere, thought, *Shut up, Troop, just shut up for a minute.*

'Straw steps out . . . taps his cleats . . . now he's back in. Gordon with the look to Williams on first . . . to the set . . . he pitches. *Out*side and low.'

Trisha moaned. The tips of her fingers were now so deeply pressed into her cheeks that her lips were pulled up in a strange distraught smile. Her heart was hammering in her chest.

'Here we go again,' Joe said. 'Gordon's ready. He fires, Strawberry swings, *and it's a long high drive to right field, if it stays fair it's gone, but it's drifting . . . it's drifting . . . driffffting . . .*'

Trisha waited, breath caught.

'Foul,' Joe said at last, and she began to breathe again. 'But that was *toooo* close. Strawberry just missed a three-run homer. It went on the wrong side of the Pesky Pole by no more than six or eight feet.'

'I'd say four feet,' Troop added helpfully.

'I'd say you've got *stinky* feet,' Trisha whispered. 'Come on, Tom, come on, *please.*' But he wouldn't; she knew that now for sure. Just this close and no closer.

Still, she could see him. Not all tall and ginky-looking like Randy Johnson, not all short and tubby-looking like Rich Garces. Medium height, trim . . . and handsome. *Very* handsome, especially with his cap on, shading his eyes . . . except her father said almost all ballplayers were handsome. 'It comes with the genes,' he told her, then added: 'Of course a lot of them have nothing upstairs, so it all balances out.' But Tom Gordon's looks weren't the thing. It was the stillness before he pitched which had first caught her eye and her admiration. He didn't stalk around the mound like some of them did, or bend to fiddle with his shoes, or pick up the rosin bag and then toss it back down in a little flump of white dust. No, Number 36 simply waited for the batter to finish all of *his* fiddle-de-diddling. He was so still in his bright white uniform as he waited for the batter to be ready. And then, of course, there was the thing he did whenever he succeeded in getting the save. That thing as he left the mound. She loved that.

'Gordon winds and fires . . . and it's in the dirt! Veritek blocked it with his body and that saved a run. The *tying* run.'

'Stone the crows!' Troop said.

Joe didn't even try to dignify that one. 'Gordon takes a deep breath out on the mound. Strawberry stands in. Gordon wheels . . . deals . . . *high*.'

A storm of booing rose in Trisha's ears like an ill wind.

'Thirty thousand or so umps in the stands didn't agree with that one, Joe,' Troop remarked.

'True, but Larry Barnett behind the plate's got the final say and Barnett said it was high. The count runs full to Darryl Strawberry. Three and two.'

In the background the rhythmic clapping of the fans swelled. Their voices filled the air, filled her head. She knocked on the wood of the tree-trunk without realizing she was doing it.

'The crowd's on its feet,' Joe Castiglione said, 'all thirty thousand of them, because no one has left the joint tonight.'

'Maybe one or two,' Troop said. Trisha took no notice. Neither did Joe.

'Gordon to the belt.'

Yes, she could see him at the belt, hands together now, no longer facing home plate directly but looking in over his left shoulder.

'Gordon into the motion.'

She could see this, too: the left foot coming back toward the planting right foot as the hands – one wearing the glove, one holding the ball – rose to the sternum; she could even see Bernie Williams, off with the pitch, streaking for second, but Tom Gordon took no notice and even in motion

71

his essential stillness remained, his eyes on Jason Veritek's mitt, hung behind the plate low and toward the outside corner.

'Gordon delivers *the three . . . two . . . pitch . . . AND—*'

The crowd told her, the sudden joyous thunder of the crowd.

'*Strike three called!*' Joe was nearly screaming. '*Oh my goodness, he threw the curve on three and two and froze Strawberry! The Red Sox win five to four over the Yankees and Tom Gordon gets his eighteenth save!*' His voice dropped into a more normal register. 'Gordon's teammates head for the mound with Mo Vaughn pumping his fist in the air and leading the charge, but before Vaughn gets there, it's Gordon with the quick gesture, the one the fans have gotten to know very well in just the short time he's been the Sox closer.'

Trisha burst into tears. She pushed the power button on the Walkman and then just sat there on the damp ground with her back against the tree-trunk and her legs spread and the blue poncho hanging between them in its hula-skirt tatters. She cried harder than she had since first realizing for sure that she was lost, but this time she cried in relief. She was lost but would be found. She was sure of it. Tom Gordon had gotten the save and so would she.

Still crying, she took off the poncho, spread it on the ground as far under the fallen tree as she thought she could wriggle, and then eased to her left until she was on the plastic. She did this with very little awareness. Most of her was still at Fenway Park, seeing the umpire ringing Strawberry up, seeing Mo Vaughn starting for the mound to congratulate Tom Gordon; she could see Nomar Garciaparra trotting in from short, John Valentin from third,

72

and Mark Lemke from second to do the same. But before they got to him, Gordon did what he always did when he secured the save: pointed at the sky. Just one quick point of the finger.

Trisha tucked her Walkman back into her pack, but before she put her head down on her outstretched arm she pointed briefly up, the way Gordon did. And why not? *Something* had brought her through the day, after all, horrible as it had been. And when you pointed, the something felt like God. You couldn't point to dumb luck or the Subaudible, after all.

Doing this made her feel better and worse – better because it felt more like praying than actual words would have done, worse because it made her feel really lonely for the first time that day; pointing like Tom Gordon made her feel lost in some heretofore unsuspected fashion. The voices which had poured out of the Walkman's earbuds and filled her head seemed dreamlike now, the voices of ghosts. She shivered at that, not wanting to think about ghosts out here, not in the woods, not cowering under a fallen tree in the dark. She missed her mother. Even more, she wanted her father. Her father would be able to get her out of here, would take her by the hand and lead her out of here. And if she got tired of walking he would carry her. He had big muscles. When she and Pete stayed weekends with him, he would still pick her up at the end of Saturday night and carry her to her little bedroom in his arms. He did that even though she was nine (and big for her age). It was her favorite part of their weekends in Malden.

Trisha discovered, with a miserable species of wonder,

that she even missed her boogery, endlessly complaining brother.

Weeping and hitching in big watery gusts of air, Trisha fell asleep. The bugs circled around her in the dark, moving closer and closer. Finally they began to light on the exposed patches of her skin, feasting on her blood and sweat.

A puff of air moved through the woods, ruffling the leaves, shaking the last of the rainwater from them. After a second or two the air fell still. Then it was not still; in the dripping quiet came the sound of twigs breaking. That stopped and there was a pause followed by a flurry of moving branches and a rough rasping sound. A crow called once, in alarm. There was a pause and then the sounds began again, moving closer to where Trisha slept with her head on her arm.

BOTTOM OF THE FOURTH

They were behind Dad's little house in Malden, just the two of them, sitting in lawn chairs that were a little too rusty, looking out over grass that was a little too long. The lawn-dwarves seemed to peer at her, smiling secret, unpleasant smiles from deep in their clumps of weeds. She was crying because Dad was being mean to her. He was never mean to her, he always hugged her and kissed the top of her head and called her sugar, but now he was, he was being mean, all because she didn't want to open the cellar bulkhead under the kitchen window and go down four steps and get him a can of beer from the case he kept down there where it was cool. She was so upset that her face must have broken out, because it was all itchy. Her arms, too.

'Baby bunting, Daddy's gone a-hunting,' he said, lean-ing toward her, and she could smell his breath. He didn't need another beer, he was drunk already, the air coming out of him smelled like yeast and dead mice. 'Why do you want to be such a little chickenguts? You don't have a single *drop* of icewater in your veins.'

Still crying, but determined to show him she did *so* have icewater in her veins — a little, anyway — she got out of the rusty lawn chair and went over to the even rustier bulkhead door. Oh, she just itched *all over*, and she didn't want to open that door because there was something awful on the other side – even the lawn-dwarves knew, you only had to look at their sly smiles to get that. She reached for the handle, though; she grasped it as behind her Dad jeered in that horrible stranger's voice to go *on,* go *on,* baby bunting, go on, *sugar,* go on, *toots,* go on and *do* it.

She pulled the door up and the stairs leading down to the cellar were gone. The stairwell itself was gone. Where it had been was a monstrous bulging wasps' nest. Hundreds of wasps were flying out of it through a black hole like the eye of a man who has died surprised, and no, it wasn't hundreds but *thousands,* plump ungainly poison factories flying straight at her. There was no time to get away, they would all sting her at once and she would die with them crawling on her skin, crawling into her *eyes,* crawling into her *mouth,* pumping her tongue full of poison on their way down her *throat*—

Trisha thought she was screaming, but when she thumped her head against the underside of the tree-trunk, showering bits of bark and moss down into her sweaty hair and waking herself up, she heard only a series of tiny, kittenish mewling sounds. They were all her locked throat would allow.

For a moment she was utterly disoriented, wondering why her bed felt so *hard,* wondering what she had thumped her head on ... was it possible she had actually gotten *under* her bed? And her skin was crawling, literally *crawling* from the dream she had just escaped, oh God what a terrible nightmare.

She rapped her head again and stuff began to come back. She wasn't on her bed or even under it. She was in the woods, lost in the woods. She had been sleeping under a tree and her skin was still crawling. Not from fear but because—

'Get off, oh you bastards get off!' she cried in a high,

frightened voice, and waved her hands rapidly back and forth in front of her eyes. Most of the minges and mosquitoes lifted from her skin and re-formed their cloud. The crawling sensation stopped but the terrible itching remained. There were no wasps, but she had been bitten just the same. Bitten in her sleep by pretty much anything that happened by and stopped for a chomp. She itched everywhere. And she needed to pee.

Trisha crawled out from under the tree-trunk, gasping and wincing. She was stiff everywhere from her tumble down the rocky slope, especially in her neck and left shoulder, and both her left arm and left leg – the limbs she had been lying on – were asleep. Numb as pegs, her mother would have said. Grownups (at least the ones in her family) had a saying for everything: numb as a peg, happy as a lark, lively as a cricket, deaf as a post, dark as the inside of a cow, dead as a—

No, she didn't want to think of that one, not now.

Trisha tried to get on her feet, couldn't, and made her way into the little crescent of clearing at a hobbling crawl. As she moved, some of the feeling started to come back into her arm and leg – those unpleasant tingling bursts of sensation. Needles and pins.

'Damn and blast,' she croaked – mostly just to hear the sound of her own voice. 'It's dark as the inside of a cow out here.'

Except, as she stopped by the brook, Trisha realized that it most surely wasn't. The little clearing was filled with moonlight, cold and lucid, strong enough to cast a firm shadow beside her and put ash-bright sparkles on the water of her little stream. The object in the sky overhead was a slightly misshapen silver stone almost too bright to look at . . . but she looked anyway, her swollen, itchy face and upcast eyes solemn. Tonight's moon was so bright that it had embarrassed all but the brightest stars into invisibility, and something about it, or about looking at it from where she was, made her feel how alone she was. Her earlier belief that she would be saved just because Tom Gordon had gotten three outs in the top of the ninth was gone – might as well knock on wood, toss salt back over your shoulder, or make the sign of the cross before you stepped into the batter's box, as Nomar Garciaparra always did. There were no cameras here, no instant replays, no cheering fans. The coldly beautiful face of the moon suggested to her that the Subaudible was more plausible after all, a God who didn't know He – or It – *was* a God, one with no interest in lost little girls, one with no real interest in anything, a knocked-out-loaded God Whose mind was like a circling cloud of bugs and Whose eye was the rapt and vacant moon.

Trisha bent over the stream to splash her throbbing face, saw her reflection, and moaned. The wasp-sting above her left cheekbone had swelled some more (perhaps she had scratched it or bumped it in her sleep), bursting through the mud she had smeared on it like a newly awakened volcano bursting through the old caked lava of its last eruption. It had mashed her eye out of shape, making it all crooked and freakish, the sort of eye that made you glance away if you saw it floating toward you – usually in the face of a mentally retarded person – on the street. The rest of her face was as bad or even worse: lumpy where she had been stung, merely swollen where mosquitoes in their hundreds had had at her while she was sleeping. The water by the bank where she crouched was relatively still, and in it she saw there was at least one mosquito still on her. It clung to the corner of her right eye, too logy to even pull its proboscis from her flesh. Another of those grownup sayings occurred to her: too stuffed to jump.

She struck at it and it burst, filling her eye with her own blood, making it sting. Trisha managed not to scream, but a wavery sound of revulsion – *mmmmmmhh* – escaped her tightly pressed lips. She looked unbelievingly at the blood on her fingers. That one mosquito could hold so much! No one would believe it!

She dipped her cupped hands into the water and washed her face. She didn't drink any, vaguely remembering someone saying that woods-water could make you sick, but the feel of it on her hot and lumpy skin was wonderful – like cold satin. She dipped up more, wetting her neck and soaking her arms to the elbow. Then she scooped up mud and began to apply it – not just on the bites this time but all over, from the round collar of her 36 GORDON shirt right up to the roots of her hair. As she did it she thought of an *I Love Lucy* episode she'd seen on Nick at Nite, Lucy and Ethel at the beauty parlor, both of them wearing these funky 1958 mudpacks, and Desi had come in and looked from one woman to the other and he had said, 'Hey Loocy, jwich one are jew?' and the audience had howled. She probably looked like that, but Trisha didn't care. There was no audience out here, no laugh-track, either, and she couldn't stand to be bitten anymore. It would drive her crazy if she was.

She applied mud for five minutes, finishing with a couple of careful dabs to the eyelids, then bent over to look at her reflection. What she saw in the relatively still water by the bank was a minstrel-show mudgirl by moonlight. Her face was a pasty gray, like a face on a vase pulled out of some archeological dig. Above it her hair stood up in a filthy spout. Her eyes were white and wet and frightened. She didn't look funny, like Lucy and Ethel getting their beauty treatments. She looked dead. Dead and badly in-barned, or whatever they called it.

Speaking to the face in the water, Trisha intoned: '*Then Little Black Sambo said,* "Please, tigers, do not take my fine new clothes."'

But that wasn't funny, either. She smeared mud up her lumpy, itchy arms, then lowered her hands toward the water, meaning to wash them off. But that was stupid. The gosh-damn old bugs would just bite her there.

The pins and needles had mostly worked out of her arm and leg; Trisha was able to squat and pee without falling over. She was also able to stand up and walk, although she grimaced with pain each time she moved her head more than a little to the right or left. She supposed she had a kind of whiplash injury, like the one Mrs. Chetwynd from up the block had gotten when some old man had rammed her car from behind as she waited for a traffic light to change. The old man hadn't been hurt a bit, but poor Mrs. Chetwynd had been in a neck brace for six weeks. Maybe they would put *her* in a neck brace when she got out of this. Maybe they would take her to a hospital in a helicopter with a red cross on the belly like in *M*A*S*H,* and—

Forget it, Trisha. It was the scary cold voice. *No neck brace for you. No helicopter ride, either.*

'Shut up,' she muttered, but the voice wouldn't.

You won't even get inbarned because they're never going to find you. You'll die out here, just wander around in these woods until you die, and the animals will come and eat your rotting body and some day some hunter will come along and find your bones.

There was something so terribly plausible about this last – she had heard similar stories on the TV news not just once but several times, it seemed – that she began to cry again. She could actually see the hunter, a man in a bright red woolen jacket and an orange cap, a man who needed a shave. Looking for a place to lie up and wait for a deer or maybe just wanting to take a leak. He sees something white and thinks at first, *Just a stone,* but as he gets closer he sees that the stone has eyesockets.

'Stop it,' she whispered, walking back to the fallen tree and the wrinkled spread remains of the poncho under it (she hated the poncho now; she didn't know why, but it seemed to symbolize everything that had gone wrong). 'Stop it, please.'

The cold voice would not. The cold voice had one more thing to say. One more thing, at least.

Or maybe you won't just die. Maybe the thing out there will kill you and eat you.

Trisha stopped by the fallen tree – one hand reached out and grasped the dead jut of a small branch – and looked around nervously. From the moment of waking all she'd really been able to think about was how badly she itched. The mud had now soothed the worst of the itching and the residual throb of the wasp-stings, and she again real-ized where she was: in the woods alone and at night.

'At least there's a moon,' she said, standing by the tree and looking nervously around her little crescent of clearing. It looked even smaller now, as if the trees and underbrush had crept in closer while she was sleeping. Crept in *slyly.*

The moonlight wasn't as good a thing as she'd thought, either. It was bright in the clearing, true, but it was a deceptive brightness that made everything look simultaneously too real and not real at all. Shadows were too black, and when a breeze stirred the trees, the shadows changed in a disquieting way.

Something twitted in the woods, seemed to choke, twitted again, and was silent.

An owl hooted, far off.

Closer to, a branch snapped.

What was that? Trisha thought, turning toward the snapping sound. Her heartbeat began to ramp up from a walk to a jog to a run. In another few seconds it would be sprinting and then *she* might be sprinting as well, panicked all over again and running like a deer in front of a forest fire.

'Nothing, it was nothing,' she said. Her voice was low and rapid . . . very much her mother's voice, although she did not know this. Nor did she know that in a motel room thirty miles from where Trisha stood by the fallen tree, her mother had sat up out of a troubled sleep, still half-dreaming with her eyes open, sure that something awful had happened to her lost daughter, or was about to happen.

It's the thing you hear, Trisha, said the cold voice. Its tone was sad on top, unspeakably gleeful underneath. *It's coming for you. It's got your scent.*

'There is no *thing*,' Trisha said in a desperate, whispery voice that broke into complete silence each time it wavered upward. 'Come on, give me a break, there is no *thing*.'

The unreliable moonlight had changed the shapes of the trees, had turned them into bone faces with black eyes. The sound of two branches rubbing together became the clotted croon of a monster. Trisha turned in a clumsy circle, trying to look everywhere at once, her eyes rolling in her muddy face.

It's a special thing, Trisha — the thing that waits for the lost ones. It lets them wander until they're good and scared — because fear makes them taste better, it sweetens the flesh — and then it comes for them. You'll see it. It'll come out of the trees any minute now. A matter of seconds, really. And when you see its face you'll go insane. If there was anyone to hear you, they'd think you were screaming. But you'll be laughing, won't you? Because that's what insane people do when their lives are ending, they laugh . . . and they laugh . . . and they laugh.

'Stop it, there is no thing, there is no thing in the woods, you stop it!'

She whispered this very fast, and the hand holding the nub of dead branch clutched it tighter and tighter until it broke with a loud report like a starter's gun. The sound made her jump and utter a little scream, but it also steadied her. She knew what it was, after all — just a branch, and one *she* had broken. She could still break branches, she still had that much control over the world. Sounds were just sounds. Shadows were just shadows. She could be afraid, she could listen to that stupid traitor of a voice if she wanted to, but there was no

(thing special thing)

in the woods. There was *wildlife,* and there was undoubtedly a spot of the old kill-or-be-killed going on out there at this very second, but there was no crea—

There is.

And there was.

Now, stopping all of her thoughts and holding her breath

without realizing it, Trisha knew with a simple cold certainty that there was. There was *something*. Inside her there were at that moment no voices, only a part of her she didn't understand, a special set of eclipsed nerves that perhaps slept in the world of houses and phones and electric lights and came fully alive only out here in the woods. That part didn't see and couldn't think, but it could feel. Now it felt something in the woods.

'Hello?' she called toward the moonlight-and-bone faces of the trees. 'Hello, is someone there?'

In the Castle View motel room Quilla had asked him to share with her, Larry McFarland sat in his pajamas on the edge of one of the twin beds with his arm around his ex-wife's shoulders. Although she wore only the thinnest of cotton nightgowns and he was pretty sure she had nothing on beneath it, and *further* although he had not had a sexual relationship with anything but his own left hand in well over a year, he felt no lust (no *immediate* lust, anyway). She was trembling all over. It felt to him as though every muscle in her back were turned inside-out.

'It's nothing,' he said. 'Just a dream. A nightmare you woke up with and turned into this feeling.'

'No,' Quilla said, shaking her head so violently that her hair whipped lightly against his cheek. 'She's in danger, I feel it. Terrible danger.' And she began to cry.

Trisha did not cry, not then. At that moment she was too scared to cry. Something watching her. *Something.*

'Hello?' she tried again. No response . . . but it was there and it was on the move now, just beyond the trees at the back of the clearing, moving from left to right. And as her eyes shifted, following nothing but moonlight and a feeling, she heard a branch crack where she was looking. There was a soft exhalation . . . or was there? Was that perhaps only a stir of wind?

You know better, the cold voice whispered, and of course she did.

'Don't hurt me,' Trisha said, and now the tears came. 'Whatever you are, please don't hurt me. I won't try to hurt you, please don't hurt me. I . . . I'm just a kid.'

The strength ran out of her legs and Trisha did not so much fall down as fold up. Still crying and shivering all over with terror, she burrowed back under the fallen tree like the small and defenseless animal that she had become. She continued begging not to be hurt almost without realizing it. She grabbed her pack and pulled it in front of her face like a shield. Big shuddery spasms wracked her body, and when another branch cracked, closer, she screamed. It wasn't in the clearing, not yet, but almost. Almost.

Was it in the trees? Moving through the interlaced branches of the trees? Something with wings, like a bat?

She peered out between the top of the pack and the curve of the sheltering tree. She saw only tangled branches against the moon-bright sky. There was no creature among them — at least not that her eyes could pick out — but now the woods had fallen completely silent. No birds called, no bugs hummed in the grass.

It was very close, whatever it was, and it was deciding. Either it would come and tear her apart, or it would move on. It wasn't a joke and it wasn't a dream. It was death and madness standing or crouching or perhaps perching just beyond the edge of the clearing. It was deciding whether to take her now . . . or to let her ripen a little while longer.

Trisha lay clutching the pack and holding her breath. After an eternity, another branch cracked, this one a little further off. Whatever it was, it was moving away.

Trisha closed her eyes. Tears slipped out from beneath her mudcaked lids and ran down her equally muddy cheeks. The corners of her mouth quivered up and down. She wished briefly that she was dead – better to be dead than have to endure such fear, better to be dead than to be lost.

Further off, another branch cracked. Leaves shook in a brief windless gust, and that was further off still. It was going, but it knew she was here now, in its woods. It would be back. Meanwhile, the night stretched out ahead of her like a thousand miles of empty road.

I'll never get to sleep. Never.

Her mother told her to pretend something when Trisha couldn't sleep. *Imagine something nice. That's the best thing you can do when the sandman's late, Trisha.*

Imagine that she was saved? No, that would only make her feel worse . . . like imagining a big glass of water when you were thirsty.

She *was* thirsty, she realized . . . dry as a bone. She guessed that was what got left over when the worst of your fear departed – that thirst. She turned her pack around with some effort and worked the buckles loose. It would have been easier if she'd been sitting up, but there was no way in the world she was coming out from under this tree again tonight, no way in the *universe*.

Unless it comes back, the cold voice said. *Unless it comes back and* drags *you out.*

She grabbed her bottle of water, had several big gulps, recapped it, restowed it. With that done, she looked longingly at the zippered pocket with her Walkman inside. She badly wanted to take it out and listen for a little while, but she should save the batteries.

Trisha rebuckled the pack's flap before she could weaken, then wrapped her arms around it again. Now that she wasn't thirsty anymore, what should she imagine? And she knew, just like that. She imagined Tom Gordon was in the clearing with her, that he was standing right over there by the stream. Tom Gordon in his home uniform; it was so white it almost glowed in the moonlight. Not really guarding her because he was just pretend . . . but *sort* of guarding her. Why not? It was her make-believe, after all.

What was that in the woods? she asked him.

Don't know, Tom replied. He sounded indifferent. Of course he could *afford* to sound indifferent, couldn't he? The real Tom Gordon was two hundred miles away in Boston, and by now probably asleep behind a locked door.

'How do you do it?' she asked, sleepy again now, so sleepy she wasn't aware that she was speaking out loud. 'What's the secret?'

Secret of what?

'Of closing,' Trisha said, her eyes closing.

She thought he would say believing in God – didn't he point to the sky every time he was successful, after all? – or believing in himself, or maybe trying your best (that was the motto of Trisha's soccer coach: 'Try your best, forget the rest'), but Number 36 said none of those things as he stood by the little stream.

You have to try to get ahead of the first hitter, was what he said. *You have to challenge him with that first pitch, throw a strike he can't hit. He comes to the plate thinking, I'm better than this guy. You have to take that idea away from him, and it's best not to wait. It's best to do it right away. Establishing that it's you who's better, that's the secret of closing.*

'What do you . . .' *like to throw on the first pitch* was the rest of the question she meant to ask, but before she could get all of it out, she was asleep. In Castle View her parents were also asleep, this time in the same narrow bed following a bout of sudden, satisfying, and totally unplanned sex. *If you had ever told me* was Quilla's last waking thought. *I never in a million years would have* was Larry's.

Of the entire family, it was Pete McFarland who slept the most uneasily in the small hours of that late spring morning; he was in the room adjoining his parents', groaning and pulling the bedclothes into a tangle as he turned restlessly from side to side. In his dreams he and his mother were arguing, walking down the trail and arguing, and at some point he turned around in disgust (or perhaps so she wouldn't have the satisfaction of seeing that he had begun to cry a little), and Trisha was gone. At this point his dream stuttered; it caught in his mind like a bone in a throat. He twisted back and forth in his bed, trying to dislodge it. The latening moon peered in at him, making the sweat on his forehead and temples gleam.

He turned and she was gone. Turned and she was gone. Turned and she was gone. There was only the empty path.

'No,' Pete muttered in his sleep, shaking his head from side to side, trying to unstick the dream, to cough it loose before it choked him. He could not. He turned and she was gone. Behind him there was only the empty path.

It was as if he had never had a sister at all.

FIFTH INNING

When Trisha woke the next morning her neck hurt so badly she could hardly turn her head, but she didn't care. The sun was up, filling the crescent-shaped clearing with early daylight. That was what she cared about. She felt reborn. She remembered waking in the night, being itchy and needing to urinate; she remembered going to the stream and putting mud on her stings and bites by moonlight; she remembered going to sleep while Tom Gordon was standing watch and explaining some of the secrets of his closer's role to her. She also remembered being terribly frightened of something in the woods, but of course nothing had been there watching; it was being alone in the dark that had frightened her, that was all.

Something deep in her mind tried to protest this, but Trisha wouldn't let it. The night was over. She wanted to look back on it no more than she wanted to go back to that rocky slope and repeat her roll down to the tree with the wasps' nest in it. It was daytime now. There would be search-parties galore and she would be saved. She knew it. She *deserved* to be saved, after spending all night alone in the woods.

She crawled out from under the tree, pushing her pack before her, got to her feet, put on her hat, and hobbled back to the stream. She washed the mud from her face and hands, looked at the cloud of minges and noseeums already re-forming around her head, and reluctantly smeared on a fresh coat of goo. As she did it she remembered one of the times she and Pepsi had played Beauty Parlor when they were little girls. They'd made such a mess of Mrs. Robichaud's makeup that Pepsi's Mom had actually screamed at them to get out of the house, not to bother washing up or trying to clean up but just to get out before she totally lost it and swatted them crosseyed. So out they had gone, all powder and rouge and eyeliner and green eyeshadow and Passion Plum lipstick, probably looking like the world's youngest stripteasers. They had gone to Trisha's house, where Quilla had first gaped, then laughed until tears rolled down her face. She had taken each little girl by the hand and led them into the bathroom, where she had given them cold cream for cleaning up.

'Spread upward *gently*, girls,' Trisha murmured now. When her face was done she rinsed her hands in the stream, ate the rest of her tuna sandwich, then half of the celery sticks. She rolled the lunchbag up with a distinct feeling of unease. Now the egg was gone, the tuna fish sandwich was gone, the chips were gone, and the Twinkies were gone. Her supplies were down to half a bottle of Surge (less, really), half a bottle of water, and a few celery sticks.

'Doesn't matter,' she said, tucking the empty lunchbag and the remaining celery sticks back in her pack. To this she added the tattered, dirty poncho. 'Doesn't matter because there's going to be search-parties galore throughout the store. One'll find me. I'll be having lunch in some diner by noon. Hamburger, fries, chocolate milk, apple pie à la mode.' Her stomach rumbled at the thought.

Once Trisha had her things packed away, she coated her hands with mud, as well. The sun had found its way into the clearing now – the day was bright, with the promise of heat – and she was moving a little more easily. She stretched, jogged in place a little to get the old blood moving, and rolled her head from side to side until the worst of the stiffness in her neck was gone. She paused a moment longer, listening for voices, for dogs, possibly for the irregular *whup-whup-whup* of helicopter blades. There was nothing except for the woodpecker, already hammering for his daily bread.

S'all right, there's plenty of time. It's June, you know. These are the longest days of the year. Follow the stream. Even if the search-parties don't find you right away, the stream will take you to people.

But as the morning wore on toward noon, the stream took her only to woods and more woods. The temperature rose. Little trickles of sweat began to cut lines through her mudpack. Bigger patches formed dark circles around the armpits of her 36 GORDON shirt; another, this one in a tree-shape, began to grow between her shoulderblades. Her hair, now so muddy it looked dirty brunette instead of blonde, hung around her face. Trisha's feelings of hope began to dissipate, and the energy with which she had set out from the clearing at seven o'clock was gone by ten. Around eleven, something happened to darken her spirits even further.

She had reached the top of a slope – this one was fairly gentle, at least, and strewn with leaves and needles – and had stopped to have a little rest when that unwelcome sense of awareness, the one which had nothing at all to do with her conscious mind, brought her on alert again. She was being watched. There was no use telling herself it wasn't true because it was.

Trisha turned slowly in a circle. She saw nothing, but the woods seemed to have hushed again – no more chipmunks bumbling and thrashing through the leaves and underbrush, no more squirrels on the far side of the stream, no more scolding jays. The woodpecker still hammered, the distant crows still cawed, but otherwise there was just her and the humming mosquitoes.

'Who's there?' she called.

There was no answer, of course, and Trisha started down the slope next to the stream, holding onto bushes because the going was slippery underfoot. *Just my imagination,* she thought . . . but she was pretty sure it wasn't.

The stream was getting narrower, and that was most certainly *not* her imagination. As she followed it down the long piny slope and then through a difficult patch of deciduous trees – too much underbrush, and too much of it thorny – it shrank steadily until it was a rill only eighteen inches or so across.

It disappeared into a thick clump of bushes. Trisha bulled her way through the close growth beside the stream instead of going around because she was afraid of losing it. Part of her knew that losing it would make no difference because it was almost certainly going nowhere *she* wanted to go, it was probably going nowhere at all, in fact, but those things seemed to make no difference. The truth was she had formed an emotional attachment to the stream – had *bonded* with it, her Mom would have said – and couldn't bear to leave it. Without it she would just be a kid wandering around in the deep woods with no plan. The very thought caused her throat to tighten and her heart to speed up.

She emerged from the bushes and the stream re-appeared. Trisha followed it with her head down and a scowl on her face, as intent as Sherlock Holmes following prints left by the Hound of the Baskervilles. She didn't notice the change in the underbrush, from bushes to ferns, nor the fact that many of the trees through which the little stream now wove its way were dead, nor the way the ground under her feet had begun to soften. All of her attention was focused on the stream. She followed it with her head down, a study in concentration.

The stream began to spread again, and for fifteen minutes or so (this was around noon) she allowed herself to hope that it wasn't going to peter out after all. Then she realized it was also growing more shallow; it really wasn't much more than a series of puddles, most dulled with pond-scum and hopping with bugs. Ten minutes or so later her sneaker disappeared through ground that wasn't solid at all but only a deceptive crust of moss over a soupy pocket of mud. It flowed over her ankle and Trisha drew her foot back with a little cry of disgust. The quick hard yank pulled her sneaker halfway off her foot. Trisha uttered another cry and held onto the trunk of a dead tree while she first wiped her foot with snatches of grass and then put her sneaker back on.

With that done she looked around and saw she had come to a kind of ghost-woods, the site of some old fire. Ahead (and already around her) was a broken maze of long-dead trees. The ground in which they stood was swampy and wet. Rising from flat pools of standing water were turtleback hummocks covered with grass and swatches of weeds. The air hummed with mosquitoes and danced with dragonflies. Now there were more woodpeckers tackhammering away, dozens of them by the sound. So many dead trees, so little time.

Trisha's brook wandered away into this morass and was lost.

'What do I do now, huh?' she asked in a teary, tired voice. 'Will somebody please tell me that?'

There were lots of places to sit and think about it; tumbles of dead trees everywhere, many still bearing scorch-marks on their pallid bodies. The first one she tried, however, gave beneath her weight and sent her spilling to the mucky ground. Trisha cried out as dampness soaked through the seat of her jeans – God, she hated having her seat get wet like that – and lurched upright again. The tree had rotted through in the damp; the freshly broken ends squirmed with woodlice. Trisha looked at them for a moment or two in revolted fascination, then walked to a second downed tree. This one she tested first. It seemed solid and she sat on it warily, looking out at the bog of broken trees, absently rubbing her sore neck and trying to decide what she should do.

Although her mind was less clear than it had been when she woke up, a *lot* less clear, there still seemed to be only two choices: stay put and hope rescue would come or keep moving and try to meet it. She supposed that staying in one place made a certain amount of sense: conservation of energy and all that. Also, without the stream, what would she be going *toward*? Nothing sure, and that was for sure. She might be heading toward civilization; she might be heading *away* from civilization. She might even get walking in a circle.

On the other hand ('There's always the other hand, sugar,' her father had once told her), there was nothing to eat here, it stank of mud and rotting trees and who knew what other gross stuff here, it was *ugly* here, it was a *bummer* here. It came to Trisha that if she stayed here and no search-party came before dark, she would be spending the night here. It was an awful idea. The little crescent-shaped clearing had been Disneyland compared to this.

She stood and peered in the direction the stream had been tending before it petered out. She was looking through a maze of gray tree-trunks and lacings of dry jutting branches, but she thought she could see green beyond them. A *rising* green. Maybe a hill. And more checker-berries? Hey, why not? She had already passed several more clumps of bushes loaded with them. She should have picked them and put them in her pack, but she had been concentrating so hard on the stream that it just hadn't occurred to her to do so. Now, however, the stream was gone and she was hungry again. Not *starving* (not yet, at least), but hungry, sure.

Trisha took two steps forward, tested a patch of soft ground, and watched with profound misgivings as water promptly seeped up around the toe of her sneaker. Was she going in there, then? Simply because she *thought* she saw the other side?

'There could be quicksand,' she muttered.

That's right! the cold voice agreed at once. It sounded amused. *Quicksand! Alligators! Not to mention little gray X-Files men with probes to stick up your butt!*

Trisha gave back the pair of steps she had taken and sat down again. She was gnawing at her lower lip without realizing it. She now hardly noticed the bugs swarming around her. Go or stay? Stay or go?

What got her going ten minutes or so later was blind hope . . . and the thought of berries. Hell, she was ready to try the leaves now, too. Trisha saw herself picking bright red berries on the slope of a pleasant green hill, looking like a girl in a schoolbook illustration (she had forgotten the mudpack on her face and the snarled, dirty spout of her hair). She saw herself picking her way to the crest of the hill, filling her pack with checkerberries . . . finally reaching the top, looking down, seeing . . .

A road. I see a dirt road with fences on both sides . . . horses grazing . . . and a barn in the distance. A red one with white trim.

Crazy! Totally bazonka!

Or was it? What if she was sitting half an hour's walk from safety, still lost because she was afraid of a little goo?

'Okay,' she said, standing up again and nervously re-adjusting the straps of her pack. 'Okay, berries ho. But if it gets too gross, I'm going back.' She gave the straps one final tug and started forward again, walking slowly over the increasingly wet ground, testing each step as she went, detouring around the skeletal standing trees and the fallen tangles of deadwood.

Eventually – it might have been half an hour after starting forward again, it might have been forty-five minutes – Trisha discovered what thousands (perhaps even millions) of men and women before her have discovered: by the time it gets too gross, it's often also too late to go back. She stepped from an oozy but stable patch of ground onto a hummock that wasn't a hummock at all but only a disguise. Her foot went into a cold, viscous substance that was too thick to be water and too thin to be mud. She tilted, grabbed a jutting dead branch, screamed in fright and vexation when it snapped off in her hand. She fell forward into long grass that hopped with bugs. She got a knee under her and yanked her foot back. It came with a loud sucking *plop,* but her sneaker stayed down there someplace.

'No!' she yelled, loud enough to scare a big white bird into flight. It exploded upward, trailing long legs behind it as it became airborne. In another place and time, Trisha would have stared at this exotic apparition with breathless wonder, but now the bird barely registered. She turned around on her knees, her right leg covered with shining black muck up to the knee, and plunged her arm into the water-welling hole which had temporarily swallowed her foot.

'You can't have it!' she shouted furiously. 'It's mine and *you . . . can't . . . HAVE IT!'*

She felt around in the cold murk, fingers tearing through membranes of roots or dodging between those too thick to tear. Something that felt alive pressed briefly against her palm, and then was gone. A moment later her hand closed over her sneaker and she pulled it out. She looked at it – a black mudshoe just right for an all-over-mudgirl, the very thing, the total puppy-shits, Pepsi would have said – and began to cry again. She lifted the sneaker up, tilted it, and a stream of grunge ran out of it. That made her laugh. For a minute or so she sat on the hummock with her legs crossed and the rescued sneaker in her lap, laughing and crying at the center of a black orbiting universe of bugs while the dead trees stood sentinel all around her and the crickets hummed.

At last her weeping tapered to sniffles, her laughter to choked and somehow humorless giggles. She tore handfuls of grass out of the hummock and wiped the outside of the sneaker as well as she could. Then she opened her pack, tore up the empty lunchbag, and used the pieces as towels to swab out the inside. These pieces she balled up and threw indifferently behind her. If someone wanted to arrest her for littering this butt-ugly, bad-smelling place, just let them.

She stood up, still holding the rescued sneaker in her hand, and looked ahead. 'Oh fuck,' Trisha croaked.

It was the first time in her life she had said that particular word out loud. (Pepsi said it sometimes, but Pepsi was Pepsi.) She could now more clearly see the green she had mistaken for a hill. It was hummocks, that was all, just more hummocks. Between them was more standing, stagnant water and more trees, most dead but some with fluffs of green at the top. She could hear frogs croaking. No hill. From bog to swamp, bad to worse.

She turned and looked back but could no longer tell where she had entered this purgatorial zone. If she'd thought to mark the place with something bright – a piece of her nasty old shredded poncho, say – she might have gone back. But she hadn't, and that was that.

You can go back anyway – you know the general direction.

Maybe, but she wasn't going to follow the kind of thinking that had gotten her into this mess in the first place.

Trisha turned toward the hummocks and the bleary glints of sun on scummy standing water. Plenty of trees to hold onto, and the swamp had to end *somewhere,* didn't it?

You're crazy to even think about it.

Sure. It was a crazy situation.

Trisha stood a moment longer, her thoughts now going to Tom Gordon and that special stillness of his – it was how he stood on the mound, watching one of the Red Sox catchers, Hatteberg or Veritek, flash the signs. So still (the way she was standing now), all of that deep stillness seeming to somehow spin out around him from the shoulders. And then to the set and the motion.

He's got icewater in his veins, her Dad said.

She wanted to get out of here, out of this nasty swamp to start with and then out of the damned woods altogether; wanted to get back to where there were people and stores and malls and phones and policemen who would help you if you lost your way. And she thought she could. If she could be brave. If she had just a little of the old icewater in her veins.

Breaking out of her own stillness, Trisha took off her other Reebok and knotted the laces of both sneakers together. She hung them around her neck like cuckoo-clock pendulums, debated over her socks, and decided to leave them on as a kind of compromise (*as an oog-shield* was the thought which actually went through her mind). She rolled the cuffs of her jeans up to her knees, then took a deep breath and let it out.

'McFarland winds, McFarland pitches,' she said. She reset-tled her Sox cap (backward this time, because backward was cool) and started moving again.

Trisha stepped from hummock to hummock with careful deliberation, looking up frequently in snatching little glances, setting a landmark and then moving toward it, just as she had yesterday. *Only today I'm not going to panic and run,* she thought. *Today I've got icewater in my veins.*

An hour passed, then two. Instead of firming, the ground grew boggier. Finally there was no solid ground at all, except for the hummocks. Trisha went from one to the next, steadying herself with branches and bushes where she could, holding her arms out for balance like a tightrope walker where there was nothing good to hold onto. Finally she came to a place where there was no hummock within jumping distance. She took a moment to steel herself and then stepped into the stagnant water, startling up a cloud of waterbugs and releasing a stench of peaty decay. The water was not quite up to her knees. The stuff her feet were sinking into felt like cold, lumpy jelly. Yellowish bubbles rose in the disturbed water; swirling in them were black fragments of who knew what.

'Gross,' she moaned, moving forward toward the nearest hummock. 'Oh, gross. Gross–gross–gross. Gag a maggot.'

She walked in lurching forward strides, each ending in a hard yank as she pulled her foot free. She tried not to think of what would happen if she couldn't do that, if she got stuck in the bottom ooze and started to sink.

'Gross–gross–gross.' It had become a chant. Sweat ran down her face in warm droplets and stung in her eyes. The crickets seemed stuck on one high endless note: *reeeeeeeee.* Ahead of her, on the hummock which was her next stop, three frogs jumped out of the grass and into the water, *plip-plip-plop.*

'Bud–Why–Zer,' Trisha said, and smiled wanly.

There were tadpoles by the thousands swimming in the

yellow-black murk around her. As she looked down at them one of her feet encountered something hard and covered with slime — a log, maybe. Trisha managed to flounder over it without falling and reach the hummock. Gasping, she pulled herself up and looked anxiously at her mud-slimy feet and legs, half-expecting to see bloodsuckers or something even worse squirming all over them. There was nothing awful (that she could see, at least), but she was covered in crud right up to her knees. She peeled off her socks, which were black, and the white skin beneath looked more like socks than her socks did. This caused Trisha to laugh maniacally. She lay back on her elbows and howled at the sky, not wanting to laugh like that, like

(*insane people*)

a total idiot, but for awhile she couldn't stop. When she was finally able to, she wrung her socks out, put them back on, and got up. She stood with her hand shielding her eyes, picked out a tree with a large lower branch broken off and dangling in the water, and made that her next goal.

'McFarland winds, McFarland pitches,' she said tiredly, and started off again. She was no longer thinking about berries; all she wanted now was to get out of here in one piece.

There is a point at which people who are cast upon their own resources stop living and begin merely surviving. The body, with all its freshest sources of energy exhausted, falls back on stored calories. Sharpness of thought begins to dull. Perception begins to both narrow and grow perversely bright. Things get wiggy around the edges. Trisha McFarland approached this borderline between life and survival as her second afternoon in the woods wore on.

That she was now moving due west did not trouble her

much; she thought (probably correctly) that moving consistently in one direction was good, the best she could do. She was hungry but for the most part not very aware of it; she was concentrating too fiercely on keeping to a straight line. If she started to wander off to the left or right, she might still be in this stinkhole when it started to get dark, and she couldn't stand that idea. Once she did stop to drink from her water bottle, and around four o'clock she drank the rest of her Surge almost without realizing it.

The dead trees began to look less and less like trees and more and more like gaunt sentinels standing with their gnarled feet in the still black water. *Be seeing faces in them again pretty soon,* she thought. While wading past one of these trees (there were no hummocks for almost thirty feet in any direction), she tripped over another submerged root or branch and this time sprawled full-length, splashing and gasping. She got a mouthful of gritty, silty water and spat it out with a cry. She could see her hands in the dark water. They looked yellowish and tallowy, like things long drowned. She pulled them out and held them up.

'I'm all right,' Trisha said rapidly, and she was almost aware of crossing some vital line; could almost feel herself going over into some other country where the language was different and the money was funny. Things were changing. But—

'I'm all right. Yeah, I'm all right.' And her pack was still dry. That was important because her Walkman was inside, and now her Walkman was her only link to the world.

Filthy, now soaked all down her front, Trisha pushed onward. The new landmark was a dead tree that split halfway up and became a black letter Y against the declining sun. She moved toward it. She came to a hummock, glanced at it briefly, and waded on through the water instead. Why bother? Wading was quicker. Her revulsion at the cold decayed jelly on the bottom had faded. You could get used to anything, if you had to. She knew that now.

Not long after taking her first spill, Trisha began passing the time of day with Tom Gordon. At first this seemed strange – weird, even – but as the long hours of late afternoon went by, she lost her self-consciousness and chattered away quite naturally, telling him which landmark she was heading for next, explaining to him that a fire had probably caused this swamp, assuring him that they would be out soon, it couldn't go on like this forever. She was telling him that she hoped the Red Sox would score about twenty runs in the game tonight so he could take it easy out there in the bullpen when she suddenly broke off.

'Do you hear something?' she asked.

She didn't know about Tom, but *she* did: the steady whapping pulse of helicopter blades. Distant but unmistakable. Trisha was resting on a hummock when she heard the sound. She jumped to her feet and turned in a complete circle, hand up and shading her eyes, squinting at the horizon. She saw nothing, and before long the sound faded.

'Spaghetti,' she said disconsolately. But at least they were looking. She slapped a mosquito on her neck and got moving again.

Ten or fifteen minutes later she was standing on the half-submerged root of a tree in her filthy, unraveling stockings and looking ahead, both wondering and puzzled. Beyond the straggling line of broken trees where she now was, the bog opened out into a flat, stagnant pond. Running across the center were more hummocks, but these were brown and seemed made of broken twigs and gnawed branches. Sitting on top of several and staring at her were half a dozen fat brown animals.

Slowly the lines on Trisha's forehead smoothed out as she realized what they were. She forgot all about being in the swamp, about being wet and muddy and tired, about being lost.

'Tom,' she whispered a little breathlessly. 'Those're beavers! Beavers sitting on beaver-houses or beaver tepees or whatever you call them. They are, aren't they?'

She stood on tiptoes, holding the trunk of the tree for balance, staring and delighted. Beavers lounging on top of their stick-houses . . . and were they watching her? She thought they were, especially the one in the middle. He was bigger than the others, and it seemed to Trisha that his black eyes never left her face. He appeared to have whiskers, and his fur was a luxuriant dark brown, shading almost to auburn around his plump haunches. Looking at him made her think of the illustrations in *The Wind in the Willows*.

Finally Trisha stepped off the root and got moving again, her shadow trailing out long behind her. At once the Head Beaver (so she thought him) got up, backed away until his hindquarters were in the water, and slapped down smartly with his tail. It made a whacking sound that was incredibly loud in the still hot air. A moment later they were all diving off the stick-houses, going into the water in unison. It was like watching an aqua-diving team. Trisha gazed at them with her hands clasped against her breastbone and a big grin on her face. It was one of the most amazing things she had ever seen in her life, and she understood that she'd never be able to explain why, or how the Head Beaver had looked like a wise old schoolmaster or something.

'Tom, look!' She pointed, laughing. 'Look at the water! There they go! Yeah, baby!'

Half a dozen Vs formed in the murky water, moving away from the stick-houses in bow-waves. Then they were gone and Trisha started moving again. Her current landmark was an extra-large hummock with dark green ferns growing all over it like wild hair. She approached it along a gradual arc instead of walking in a straight line. Seeing the beavers had been great – totally ghetto, in Pepsi-ese – but she had no desire to encounter one while it was swimming underwater. She had seen enough pictures to know that even little beavers had big teeth. For awhile Trisha uttered a shriek each time a submerged bit of grass or weed brushed against her, sure it was the Head Beaver (or one of his minions), wanting her out of the neighborhood.

Keeping the beaver-condos always on her right, she approached the extra-large hummock – and as she drew closer, a sense of hopeful excitement began to grow in her. Those dark green ferns weren't *just* ferns, she thought; she had been fiddleheading with her mother and grandmother three springs in a row, and she thought those were fiddle-heads. Fiddleheads were over in Sanford – had been for at least a month – but her mother had told her they came into season quite a bit later inland, almost up until July in especially marshy places. It was hard to believe anything good could come out of this smelly patch of creation, but the closer Trisha got, the surer she became. And fiddleheads weren't just good; fiddleheads were *delicious*. Even Pete, who had never met a green vegetable he liked (except for frozen Birds Eye peas nuked in the microwave), ate fiddleheads.

She told herself not to expect too much, but five minutes after the possibility first occurred to her, Trisha was sure. That was no mere hummock up ahead; that was Fiddlehead Island! Except maybe, she thought as she drew closer, wading slowly through water that was now thigh-deep, Bug Island would be a better name. There were *lots* of bugs out here, of course, but she kept replenishing her mudpack and had pretty much forgotten about them until now. The air over Fiddlehead Island absolutely *shimmered* with them, and not just minges and noseeums. There were a gazillion flies as well. As she drew closer she could hear their somnolent, somehow shiny buzz.

She was still half a dozen steps away from the first bunches of plump furled greens when she stopped, hardly aware of her feet settling into the muddy mulch under the water. The greenery bordering this side of the tussock was shredded and torn; here and there soggy uprooted bunches of fiddleheads still floated on the black water. Further up she could see bright red splashes on the green.

'I don't like this,' she murmured, and when she next moved it was to her left instead of straight ahead. Fiddleheads were fine, but there was something dead or badly wounded up there. Maybe the beavers fought with each other for mates or something. She wasn't yet hungry enough to dare meeting a wounded beaver while gathering an early supper. That would be a good way to lose a hand or an eye.

Halfway around Fiddlehead Island, Trisha stopped again.

She didn't want to look, but at first she couldn't look away. 'Hey, Tom,' she said in a high trembling voice. 'Oh hey, bad.'

It was the severed head of a small deer. It had rolled down the slope of the tussock, leaving a trail of blood and matted fiddlehead ferns behind. It now lay upside down at the water's edge. Its eyes shimmered with nits. Regiments of flies had alit on the ragged stump of its neck. They hummed like a small motor.

'I see its tongue,' she said, and her voice was far away, down an echoing hallway. The gold suntrack on the water was suddenly too bright, and she felt herself swaying on the edge of a faint.

'No,' she whispered. '*No*, don't let me, I *can't*.'

This time her voice, although lower, seemed closer and more *there*. The light looked almost normal again. Thank God – the last thing she wanted was to faint while standing almost waist-deep in stagnant, mucky water. No fiddle-heads, but no fainting, either. It almost balanced.

She pushed ahead, walking faster and being less careful about testing her footing before settling her weight. She moved in an exaggerated side-to-side motion, hips rotating, arms going back and forth across her body in short arcs. She guessed if she had a leotard on, she'd look like the guest of the day on *Workout with Wendy*. Say, everybody, today we're doing some brand-new exercises. I call this one 'Getting away from the torn-off deer's head.' Pump those hips, flex those butts, work those shoulders!

She kept her eyes pointed forward, but there was no way not to hear the heavy, somehow self-satisfied drone of the flies. What had done it? Not a beaver, that was for sure.

No beaver ever tore a deer's head off, no matter how sharp its teeth were.

You know what it was, the cold voice told her. *It was the thing. The special thing. The one that's watching you right now.*

'Nothing's watching me, that's crap,' she panted. She risked a glance over her shoulder and was glad to see Fiddlehead Island falling behind. Not quite fast enough, though. She glimpsed the head lying at the edge of the water one last time, the brown thing wearing a buzzing black necklace. 'That's crap, isn't it, Tom?'

But Tom didn't answer. Tom *couldn't* answer. Tom was probably at Fenway Park by now, joking around with his fellow teammates and putting on his bright white home uniform. The Tom Gordon walking through the bog with her – this endless bog – was just a little homeopathic cure for loneliness. She was on her own.

Except you're not, sugar. You're not alone at all.

Trisha was terribly afraid the cold voice, although not her friend, was telling the truth. That feeling of being watched had come back, and stronger than ever. She tried to dismiss it as nerves (anyone would have jumpy nerves after seeing that torn-off head) and had almost succeeded when she came to a tree which had been scored with half a dozen diagonal cuts through its old dead bark. It was as if something very big and in a very bad frame of mind had slashed at it on its way by.

'Oh my God,' she said. 'Those are claw-marks.'

It's up ahead, Trisha. Up ahead waiting for you, claws and all.

Trisha could see more standing water, more hummocks, what looked like another green, rising hill (but she had been fooled that way before). She saw no beast . . . but of course she wouldn't, would she? The beast would do whatever beasts did while they were waiting to spring, there was a word for it but she was too tired and scared and generally miserable to think of it . . .

They lurk, said the cold voice. *That's what they do, they lurk. Yeah, baby. Especially special ones like your new friend.*

'Lurk,' Trisha croaked. 'Yes, that's the word. Thank you.' And then she started forward again because it was too far to go back. Even if something really was waiting up ahead to kill her, it was too far to go back.

This time what looked like solid ground turned out to *be* solid ground. At first Trisha wouldn't let herself believe it, but as she drew closer and still couldn't see water cutting through that mass of green bushes and scrubby trees, she began to hope. The water in which she was wading was shallower, too: only up to mid-shin instead of to her knees or thighs. And there were more fiddleheads growing on at least two of the hummocks. Not as many as there had been back on Fiddlehead Island, but she picked what there were and gobbled them down. They were sweet, with a faintly acrid aftertaste. It was a *green* taste, and Trisha thought it absolutely delicious. She would have picked more and stored them in her pack if there had been more, but there weren't. Instead of mourning this, she relished what she had with a child's single-mindedness. There was enough for now; she would worry about later later. She snacked her way toward solid ground, biting off the furled nubbins and then nibbling on the stalks. She was hardly aware of wading through the bog now; her revulsion had passed.

As she reached toward the last few fiddleheads growing

on the second hummock, her hand froze. She heard the somnolent buzzing of flies again. It was a lot louder this time. Trisha would have angled away from it if she could, but as the swamp ran out it had become choked with dead branches and drowned bushes. There seemed to be only a single halfway-clear channel through this mess, and she'd have to take it unless she wanted to spend an extra two hours struggling over submerged barriers and maybe cutting her feet up in the process.

Even in this channel, she was forced to clamber over one downed tree. It had fallen just recently, and 'fallen' was really the wrong word. Trisha could see more slash-marks in its bark, and although the butt-end of its trunk was lost in a tangle of bushes, she could see how fresh and white the wood of the stump was. The tree had gotten in something's way, and so the something had simply pushed it over, snapping it like a toothpick.

The buzzing grew louder still. The rest of the deer — most of it, anyway — was lying at the foot of an extravagant splurge of fiddleheads near the spot where Trisha finally climbed wearily out of the swamp. It lay in two pieces which were connected by a fly-shining snarl of intestines. One of its legs had been torn off and stood propped against the trunk of a nearby tree like a walking stick.

Trisha put the back of her right hand over her mouth and hurried rapidly on, making weird little *urk-urk* sounds as she went and trying with all her might not to upchuck. The thing that had killed the deer *wanted* her to upchuck, maybe. Was that possible? The rational part of her mind (and there was still quite a lot of it) said no, but it seemed to her that *something* had deliberately polluted the two biggest, lushest growths of fiddleheads in the bog with a deer's mangled body. And if it had done that, was it impossible to believe it might try to make her throw up the little nourishment she *had* managed to scrounge?

Yes. It is. You're being a dork. Forget it. And don't upchuck, for heaven's sake!

The *urk-urk* noises — they were like big, meaty hiccups — began to space themselves out as she walked west (keeping on a westward course was easy now, with the sun low in the sky) and the sound of the flies began to recede. When it was entirely gone, Trisha stopped, took off her socks, then slipped her sneakers back on. She wrung the socks out again, then held them up and looked at them. She could remember putting them on in her Sanford bedroom, just sitting there on the end of the bed and putting them on while she sang 'Put your arms around me . . . cuz I gotta get next to you' under her breath. That was Boyz To Da Maxx; she and Pepsi thought Boyz To Da Maxx were yummy, especially Adam. She remembered the patch of sun on the floor. She remembered her *Titanic* poster on the wall. This memory of putting on her socks in her bedroom was very clear but very distant. She guessed it was the way old people like Grampa remembered things which had happened when they were kids. Now the socks were little more than holes held together by strings, and that made her feel like crying again (probably because she herself felt like holes held together by strings), but she controlled that, too. She rolled the socks and put them in her pack.

She was re-fastening the buckles when she heard the *whup-whup-whup* of helicopter rotor-blades again. This time they sounded much closer. Trisha bounded to her feet and turned around with her wet clothes flapping. And there, off in the east, black against the blue sky, were two shapes. They reminded her a little bit of the dragonflies back there in Dead Deer Swamp. There was no sense waving and shouting, they were about a billion miles away, but she did it anyway – she couldn't help herself. At last, when her throat was raw, she quit.

'Look, Tom,' she said, following them wistfully from left to right . . . north to south, that would be. 'Look, they're trying to find me. If they'd just come a little bit closer . . .'

But they didn't. The distant helicopters disappeared behind the bulk of the forest. Trisha stood where she was, not moving until the sound of the rotors had faded into the steady hum of the crickets. Then she fetched a deep sigh and knelt to tie her sneakers. She couldn't feel anything watching her anymore, that was one thing—

Oh you liar, the cold voice said. It was amused. *You little liar you.*

But she *wasn't* lying, at least not on purpose. She was so tired and so mixed up she wasn't sure *what* she felt . . . except still hungry and thirsty. Now that she was out of the muck and the goo (and away from the torn corpse of the deer), she felt hunger and thirst very clearly. It crossed her mind to go back and pick more of the fiddleheads after all – she could steer clear of the deer's body and the goriest, bloodiest places, surely.

She thought of Pepsi, who was sometimes impatient with Trisha if Trisha scraped her knee while they were rollerblading or fell while they were tree-climbing. If she saw tears welling in Trisha's eyes, Pepsi was apt to say, 'Don't go all girly on me, McFarland.' God knew she couldn't afford to go all girly about a dead deer, not in a situation like this, but . . .

. . . but she was afraid that the thing which had killed the deer might still be there, watching and waiting. Hoping she'd come back.

As for drinking the bog-water, get serious. Dirt was one thing. Dead bugs and mosquito eggs were something else. Could mosquitoes hatch in a person's stomach? Probably not. Did she want to find out for sure? *Definitely* not.

'I'll probably find some more fiddleheads, anyway,' she said. 'Right, Tom? And berries, too.' Tom didn't reply, but before she could have any second thoughts, she got moving again.

She walked west for another three hours, at first moving slowly, then able to go a little faster as she entered a more mature stretch of woods. Her legs ached and her back throbbed, but neither of these hurting places drew much of her attention. Not even her hunger occupied her mind to any real degree. As the day's light went first to golden and then to red, it was her thirst that came to dominate Trisha's thoughts. Her throat was dry and throbbing; her tongue felt like a dusty worm. She cursed herself for not having drunk from the swamp when she had the chance, and once she stopped, thinking, *Screw this, I'm going back.*

You better not try, sweetheart, said the cold voice. *You'd never find your way. Even if you were lucky enough to backtrack perfectly, it would be dark before you got there . . . and who knows what might be waiting?*

'Shut up,' she said wearily, 'just shut up, you stupid mean bitch.' But of course the stupid mean bitch was right. Trisha turned back in the direction of the sun – it was now orange – and began walking again. She was becoming actively frightened of her thirst now: if it was this bad at eight o'clock, what would it be like at midnight? Just how long could a person live without water, anyway? She couldn't remember, although she had come across that particular fun fact at some time or other – she was sure that she had. Not as long as a person could go without food, anyway. What would it be like to die of thirst?

'I'm not going to die of thirst in the darn old woods . . . am I, Tom?' she asked, but Tom wasn't saying. The real Tom Gordon would be watching the game by now. Tim Wakefield, Boston's crafty knuckleballer, against Andy Pettitte, the Yankees' young lefthander. Trisha's throat throbbed. It was hard to swallow. She remembered how it had rained (as with her memory of sitting on the end of her bed and putting on her socks, this also seemed like a long time ago) and wished it would rain again. She would get out in it and dance with her head back and her arms out and her mouth open; she would dance like Snoopy on top of his doghouse.

Trisha plodded through pines and spruces that grew taller and better spaced as this part of the woods grew older. The light of the setting sun came slanting through the trees in dusty bars of deepening color. She would have thought the trees and the orange-red light beautiful if not for her thirst . . . and a part of her mind noted their beauty even in her physical distress. The light was too bright, though. Her temples were pounding with a headache and her throat felt like a pinhole.

In this state, she first dismissed the sound of running water as an auditory hallucination. It couldn't be real water; it was too darned convenient. Nevertheless she turned toward it, now walking southwest instead of due west, ducking under low branches and stepping over fallen logs like someone in a hypnotic trance. When the sound grew even louder – too loud to mistake for anything other than what it was – Trisha began to run. She slipped twice on the carpet of needles underfoot, and once she ran through an ugly little pocket of nettles that tore fresh cuts on her forearms and the backs of her hands, but she hardly noticed. Ten minutes after first hearing that faint rushing noise, she came to a short, steep drop-off where the bedrock emerged from the thin soil and needle carpeting of the forest floor in a series of gray stone knuckles. Below these, brawling along at a healthy clip, was a brook that made her first one seem like no more than a drip from the end of a shut-off hose.

Trisha walked along the edge of the drop with perfect unself-consciousness, although a misstep would have sent her tumbling at least twenty-five feet and likely would have killed her. Five minutes' walk upstream brought her to a kind of rough groove from the edge of the forest into the gully where the stream ran. It was a natural flume, floored with decades of fallen leaves and needles.

She sat down and hooked herself forward with her feet until she sat on top of the grooved place like a kid sitting on top of a slide. She started down, still sitting, dragging her hands and using her feet as brakes. About halfway down she started to skid. Rather than trying to stop herself – that would most likely start her somersaulting again – she lay back, laced her hands together behind her neck, closed her eyes, and hoped for the best.

The trip to the bottom was short and jolting. Trisha whammed into one jutting rock with her right hip, and another struck her laced-together fingers hard enough to numb them. If she hadn't put her hands over the top of her head, that second rock might have torn open her scalp, she thought later. Or worse. 'Don't break your fool neck' was another grownup saying she knew, this one a favorite of Gramma McFarland.

She hit bottom with a bonecrunching thud, and suddenly her sneakers were full of freezing cold water. She pulled them out, turned around, flopped onto her belly, and drank until a spike drove into her forehead the way it sometimes did when she was hot and hungry and gobbled ice cream too fast. Trisha pulled her dripping, mudstreaked face out of the stream's cold boiling course and looked up at the darkening sky, gasping and grinning blissfully. Had she ever tasted water this good? No. Had she ever tasted *anything* this good? Absolutely not. This was in a class by itself. She plunged her face back in and drank again. At last she got up on her knees, uttered a vast watery belch, and then laughed shakily. Her stomach felt swollen, tight as a drum. For the time being, at least, she wasn't even hungry.

The flume was too steep and too slippery to re-climb; she might get halfway or even most of the way up only to slide all the way back to the bottom again. The going looked fairly easy on the other side of the brook, however – steep and tree-covered but not too brushy – and there were plenty of rocks to use as stepping-stones. She could go a little way before it got too dark to see. Why not? Now that she had filled her belly with water she felt strong again, wonderfully strong. And confident. The bog was behind her and she had found another stream. A good stream.

Yes, but what about the special thing? the cold voice asked. Trisha was frightened by that voice all over again. The stuff it said was bad; that she should have discovered such a dark girl hiding inside her was even worse. *Did you forget about the special thing?*

'If there ever was a special thing,' Trisha said, 'it's gone now. Back with the deer, maybe.'

It was true, or seemed to be true. That sensation of being watched, perhaps stalked, was gone. The cold voice knew it and made no reply. Trisha found she could visualize its owner, a tough little sneery-mouthed tootsie who looked only slightly, coincidentally, like Trisha herself (the resemblance of a second cousin, perhaps). Now she was stalking away with her shoulders held stiffly high and her fists clenched, the very picture of resentment.

'Yeah, go away and stay away,' Trisha said. 'You don't scare me.' And after a pause: 'Fuck you!' There it came out of her mouth again, what Pepsi called The Terrible Effword, and Trisha wasn't sorry. She could even imagine saying it to her brother Pete if Pete started up with all his Malden crap again while they were walking home from school. Malden this and Malden that, Dad this and Dad that, and what if she just said *Hey Pete, fuck you, deal with it* instead of trying to be either all quiet and sympathetic or all bright and cheery and let's-change-the-subject? Just *Hey Pete, that's a big fuck you,* like that? Trisha saw him in her head – saw him staring at her with his jaw dropped most of the way down to his chin. The image made her giggle.

She got up, approached the water, picked out four stones that would take her across, and dropped them, one at a time, into the streambed. Once on the far side, she began to work her way down the slope.

The hillside steepened steadily and the stream grew ever noisier beside her, rolling and tumbling in its rocky bed. When Trisha came to a clearing where the ground was relatively flat, she decided to stop for the night. The air had grown thick and shadowy; if she tried to go on down the slope, she would be risking a fall. Besides, this wasn't too bad; she could see the sky, at least.

'Bugs are fierce, though,' she said, waving at the mosquitoes around her face and slapping a few more off her neck. She went to the stream to get mud, but – ha-ha, joke's on you, girl – there was no mud to get. Plenty of rocks but no mud. Trisha sat back on her heels for a moment while the minges executed complicated flying patterns around her eyes, thought things over, then nodded. She scraped the needles away from a small circle of ground with the sides of her hands, dug a little bowl in the soft earth, then used her water-bottle to fill it up from the stream. She made mud with her fingers, taking a great deal of pleasure in the process (it was Gramma Andersen she thought of, making bread in Gramma Andersen's kitchen on Saturday mornings, standing on a stool to knead the dough because the counter was so high). When she had lots of good goo she smeared it all over her face. By the time she finished this, it was almost dark.

Trisha stood up, still rubbing mud on her arms, and looked around. There was no convenient fallen tree to sleep under tonight, but about twenty yards from this side of the stream she spied a tangle of dead pine-boughs. She took these to one of the tall firs near the stream and leaned them against the trunk like upside-down fans, creating a little space she could crawl into . . . sort of a half-tent. If no wind came up to knock the branches over, she thought she would be fairly snug.

As she brought the last two over, her stomach cramped and her bowels loosened. Trisha stopped, holding a branch in each hand, waiting to see what would happen next. The cramp let go and the odd weak feeling down low inside of her passed, but she still didn't feel quite right. Fluttery. *Butterfluttery* was Gramma Andersen's word, only she used it to mean nervous and Trisha didn't feel nervous, exactly. She didn't know *how* she felt.

It was the water, the cold voice said. *Something in the water. You're poisoned, sugar. Probably be dead by morning.*

'If I am I am,'Trisha said, and added the last two branches to her makeshift shelter. 'I was so thirsty. I had to drink.'

To this there was no reply. Perhaps even the cold voice, traitor that it was, understood that much – she'd had to drink, *had* to.

She slipped off her pack, opened it, and reverently took out her Walkman. She settled the earbuds into place and pushed the power button. WCAS was still strong enough to listen to, but the signal wasn't what it had been last night. It made Trisha feel funny to think she had almost walked out of a radio station's broadcast area the way that you drove out of them when you were on a long car-trip. It made her feel funny, all right, very funny indeed. Funny in her stomach.

'All right,' Joe Castiglione said. His voice was thin,

seeming to come from a great distance. 'Mo stands in and we're ready for the bottom of the fourth.'

Suddenly the butterflutters were in her throat as well as her stomach, and those meaty hiccups – *urk-urk, urk-urk* – started again. Trisha rolled away from her shelter, lurched to her knees, and threw up into the shadows between two trees, holding onto one tree with her left hand and clutching her stomach with her right.

She stayed where she was, gasping for breath and spitting out the taste of slightly used fiddleheads – sour, acidic – while Mo fanned on three pitches. Troy O'Leary was up next.

'Well, the Red Sox have got their work cut out for them,' Troop remarked. 'They're down seven to one in the bottom of the fourth and Andy Pettitte is twirling a gem.'

'Oh *sugartit,*' Trisha said, and then vomited again. She couldn't see what was coming out, it was too dark for that and she was glad, but it felt thin, more like soup than puke. Something about the almost-rhyme of those two words, soup and puke, made her stomach immediately knot up again. She backed away from the trees between which she had thrown up, still on her knees, and then her bowels cramped again, this time more fiercely.

'*Oh SUGARTIT!*' Trisha wailed, tearing at the snap on the top of her jeans. She was sure she wasn't going to make it, absolutely positive, but in the end she was able to hold on just long enough to get her jeans and underwear yanked down and pulled out of the way. Everything down there came out in a hot, stinging rush. Trisha cried out and some bird in the dying light cried back, as if in mockery. When it was finally over and she tried to get on her feet, a wave of lightheadedness struck her. She lost her balance and plopped back down in her own hot mess.

'Lost and sitting in my own crap,' Trisha said. She began to cry again, then also to laugh as it struck her funny. *Lost and sitting in my own crap indeed,* she thought. She struggled up, crying and laughing, her jeans and underwear puddled around her ankles (the jeans were torn at both knees and stiff with mud, but at least she'd avoided dipping them in shit . . . so far, anyway). She pulled her pants off and walked to the stream, naked from the waist down and holding her Walkman in one hand. Troy O'Leary had singled around the time she lost her balance and plopped into her own poop; now as she stepped barefoot into the freezing cold stream, Jim Leyritz hit into a double play. Side retired. Utterly SECK-shoo-al.

Bending, getting water and splashing it onto her fanny and the backs of her thighs, Trisha said: 'It was the water, Tom, it was the damn old water, but what was I supposed to do? Just *look* at it?'

Her feet were completely numb by the time she stepped out of the stream; her backside was also pretty numb, but at least she was clean again. She put on her underwear and her pants and was just doing the snap on the jeans when her stomach clenched again. Trisha took two big steps back to the trees, clutched the same one, and vomited again. This time there seemed to be nothing solid in it at all; it was like ejecting two cups of hot water. She leaned forward and put her forehead against the pine tree's sticky bark. For just a moment she could imagine a sign on it, like the kind people hung over the doors of their lakeside and seaside camps: TRISHA'S PUKIN' PLACE. That made her laugh again, but it was bad laughter. And through all the air between these woods and the world she had so foolishly believed was hers, that jingle was playing again, the one that went 'Dial 1-800-54-GIANT.'

Now her bowels again, tightening and cramping.

'No,' Trisha said, with her forehead still against the tree and her eyes closed. 'No, please, no more. Help me, God. Please no more.'

Don't waste your breath, said the cold voice. *It's no good praying to the Subaudible.*

The cramp loosened. Trisha walked slowly back to her shelter on legs that felt rubbery and unstable. Her back hurt from vomiting; her stomach muscles felt oddly sprung. And her skin was hot. She thought maybe she had a fever.

Derek Lowe came in to pitch for the Red Sox. Jorge Posada greeted him with a triple into the right-field corner. Trisha crawled into her shelter, being careful not to brush any of the branches with her arm or hip. If she did that the whole thing would probably fall over. If she was caught short again (that's what her Mom called it; Pepsi called it 'having the Hershey squirts' or 'doing the outhouse polka'), she'd probably knock it all over, anyway. Meantime, though, she was in here.

Chuck Knoblauch hit what Troop called 'a towering fly ball.' Darren Bragg caught it, but Posada scored. Eight to one, Yankees. She was on a roll tonight, no doubt about it. On an absolute roll.

'Who do you call when your *wind*shield's *bust*ed?' she sang under her breath as she lay on the pine needles. '1-800-54-GI—'

A sudden spasm of the shivers took her; instead of hot

and feverish, she felt cold all over. She grabbed her muddy arms with her muddy fingers and held on, hoping the branches she had so carefully set up wouldn't all fall down on top of her.

'The water,' she moaned. 'The water, the damned old water, no more of that.'

But she knew better, and didn't need the cold voice to tell her anything. She was already thirsty again, vomiting and the aftertaste of fiddleheads had made the thirst even stronger, and she would be revisiting the stream soon enough.

She lay listening to the Red Sox. They woke up in the eighth, scoring four runs and chasing Pettitte. While the Yankees batted against Dennis Eckersley in the top of the ninth ('the Eck' was what Joe and Troop called him), Trisha gave in – she couldn't stand listening to the daffy babble of the stream any longer. Even with the Walkman's volume turned up it was there, and her tongue and throat begged for what she was hearing. She backed carefully out of the shelter, went to the stream, and drank again. It was cold and delicious, tasting not like poison but like the nectar of the gods. She crawled back to her shelter, alternately hot and cold, sweaty and shivery, and as she lay down again she thought, *I'll probably be dead by morning. Dead or so sick I'll wish I was dead.*

The Red Sox, now down by a score of eight to five, loaded the bases with just one out in the bottom of the ninth. Nomar Garciaparra hit a deep drive to center field. If it had gone out, the Sox would have won the game by a score of nine to eight. Instead, Bernie Williams made a leaping grab at the bullpen wall and snared Garciaparra's bid. One run scored on the sacrifice fly, but that was all. O'Leary came up and struck out against Mariano Rivera, completing an undistinguished night and ending the game. Trisha pushed the power button on her Walkman, saving the batteries. Then she began to cry, weakly and helplessly, with her head in her crossed arms. She was sick to her stomach and queasy in her bowels; the Sox had lost; Tom Gordon never even got in the stupid *game.* Life was the puppy-shits. She was still crying when she fell asleep.

At the Maine state police barracks in Castle Rock, a short telephone call came in just as Trisha was going against her better judgment and drinking from the stream for the second time. The caller gave his message to the operator and to the tape-recorder which preserved all incoming calls.

Call commences 2146 Hours

Caller: The girl you're looking for was snatched off the trail by Francis Raymond Mazzerole, that's M as in microscope. He's thirty-six years old, wears glasses, has short hair dyed blond. Got that?
Operator: Sir, can I ask you to—

Caller: Shut up, shut up, listen. Mazzerole is driving a blue Ford van, what I think is called an Econoline. He is in Connecticut by now at least. He is a bad scumbag. Run his record and you'll see. He'll fuck her a few days if she doesn't give him any trouble, you could have a few days, but then he'll kill her. He's done it before.

Operator: Sir, do you have a license number—

Caller: I gave you his name and what he's driving. I gave you all you need. He's done this before.

Operator: Sir—

Caller: I hope you kill him.

Call ends 2148 Hours

Traceback put the origin of the call at a pay telephone in Old Orchard Beach. No help there.

Around two o'clock the next morning – three hours after police in Massachusetts, Connecticut, New York, and New Jersey had begun looking for a blue Ford van driven by a man with short blond hair, wearing eyeglasses – Trisha awoke with more nausea and cramps. She knocked her shelter over backing out of it, fumbled her jeans and underwear down, and voided what seemed like a huge quantity of weak acid. It hurt her down there, hurt with a deep itching sting that felt like the worst case of prickly heat she'd ever had.

When that part was over she crawled back to Trisha's Pukin' Place and grabbed hold of the same tree. Her skin was hot, her hair was matted with sweat; she was also shaking all over and her teeth were chattering.

I can't vomit any more. Please God, I can't vomit any more. It'll kill me if I go on vomiting.

This was when she actually saw Tom Gordon for the first time. He was standing in the woods about fifty feet away, his white uniform seeming almost to burn in the moonlight which fell through the trees. He was wearing his glove. His right hand was behind his back and Trisha knew there was a baseball in it. He would be cupping it against his palm and twirling it in his long fingers, feeling the seams go by, stopping only when they were exactly where he wanted them and the grip was right.

'Tom,' she whispered. 'You never got a chance tonight, did you?'

Tom took no notice. He was looking in for the sign. That stillness spun out from his shoulders, enveloping him. He stood there in the moonlight, as clear as the cuts on her arms, as real as the nausea in her throat and belly, all those nasty butterflutters. He was stillness waiting for the sign. Not *perfect* stillness, there was that hand behind his back turning the ball and turning the ball, searching for the best grip, but all stillness where you could see; yeah, baby, stillness waiting for the sign. Trisha wondered if she could do that – just let the shakes run off her like water off a duck's back and be still and conceal the churning inside her.

She held onto the tree and tried. It didn't happen all at once (good things never did, her Dad said), but it did happen: quiet inside, blessed stillness. She stayed that way for a long time. Did the batter want to step out because he thought she was taking too long between pitches? Fine. It was nothing to her, one way or the other. She was only stillness, stillness waiting for the right sign and the right grip on the ball. Stillness came from the shoulders, it spun out from there, it cooled you and focused you.

The shivers eased, then stopped entirely. At some point

she realized that her stomach had also settled. Her bowels were still crampy, but not as bad now. The moon was down. Tom Gordon was gone. Of course he had never really been there at all, she knew that, but—

'He sure looked real that time,' she croaked. 'Real as real. Wow.'

She got up and walked slowly back to the tree where her shelter had been. Although she wanted nothing except to huddle on the pine needles and go to sleep, she set up the fans of branches again, then crawled in behind them. Five minutes later she was dead to the world. As she slept, something came and watched her. It watched for a long time. It was not until light began to line the horizon in the east that it went away . . . and it did not go far.

SIXTH INNING

When Trisha woke up, the birds were singing confidently. The light was strong and bright, the way it looked at mid-morning. She might have slept even longer, but hunger wouldn't allow it. She roared with a vast emptiness from the top of her throat all the way down to her knees. And in the very middle it hurt, actually *hurt*. It was as if she were being pinched somewhere inside. The feeling frightened her. She had been hungry before, but never hungry enough for it to hurt this way.

She backed out of her shelter, knocking it over again, got to her feet, and hobbled to the stream with her hands planted in the small of her back. She probably looked like Pepsi Robichaud's grandmother, the one who was deaf and had arthritis so bad she had to use a walker. Granny Grunt, Pepsi called her.

Trisha got down on her knees, planted her hands, and drank like a horse at a trough. If the water made her sick again, and it probably would, so be it. She had to put *something* in her stomach.

She got up, looked dully around her, hitched up her jeans (they had been okay when she put them on, long ago and far away in her Sanford bedroom, but they were loose now), then started downhill along the course of the stream. She no longer had any real hope that it would take her out, but at least she could put some distance between her and Trisha's Pukin' Place; she could do that much.

She had gotten perhaps a hundred paces when the tough tootsie spoke up. *Forgot something, didn't you, sugar?* Today the tough tootsie also sounded like a getting-tired tootsie, but her voice was as cold and ironic as ever. Not to mention correct. Trisha stood where she was for a moment with her head down and her hair hanging, then turned around and labored uphill to her little camp of the night before. She had to stop twice on the way and give her pounding heart a chance to slow down; she was appalled by how little strength she had left.

She filled her water-bottle, stuffed it and the shredded remains of her poncho into her pack, gave a tearful sigh at the pack's weight when she lifted it (the damned thing was all but *empty*, for goodness' sake), and then set off again. She walked slowly, almost plodding now, and although the going was downhill she still had to stop and rest every fifteen minutes or so. Her head throbbed. All the world's colors looked too bright, and when a bluejay called from a branch overhead, the sound seemed to punch into her ears like needles. She pretended Tom Gordon was with her, keeping her company, and then after awhile she didn't have to pretend anymore. He walked along beside her, and although she knew he was a hallucination, he looked as real by daylight as he had by moonlight.

Around noon, Trisha stumbled over a rock and sprawled full-length in a brambly snarl of bushes. She lay there with the breath knocked out of her and her heart hammering so hard it made white lights in front of her eyes. The first time she attempted to drag herself back to open ground she couldn't do it. She waited, rested, tried for stillness with her eyes half-closed, and then went for it again. This time she pulled herself free, but when she tried to get up, her legs wouldn't support her. No wonder, either, not really. Over the last forty-eight hours she'd had nothing to eat but a hardboiled egg, a tuna sandwich, two Twinkies, and a few fiddleheads. She'd also had diarrhea and vomiting.

'I'm going to die, Tom, aren't I?' she asked. Her voice was calm, lucid.

There was no answer. Trisha raised her head and looked around. Number 36 was gone. Trisha dragged herself over to the stream and had a drink. The water didn't seem to be bothering her stomach and bowels anymore. She didn't know if that meant she was getting used to it or just that her body had given up trying to rid itself of the bad stuff, the impurities.

Trisha sat up, wiped her dripping mouth, and looked northwest, along the course of the stream. The terrain up ahead was moderating, and the old forest seemed to be changing once again, the firs giving way to smaller, younger trees – your basic forest clenches and tangles, in other words, with plenty of underbrush clogging up any easy way through. She didn't know how long she could continue in that direction. And if she tried to walk in the stream, she guessed that the current would bowl her over. There were no helicopters, no barking dogs. She had an idea she could hear those sounds if she wanted to, just as she could see Tom Gordon if she wanted to, so it was best not to think in that direction. If any sounds surprised her, they might be real.

Trisha didn't think any sounds would surprise her.

'I'm going to die in the woods.' Not a question this time.

Her face twisted into an expression of sorrow, but there were no tears. She held out her hands and looked at them. They were trembling. At last she got to her feet and began to walk again. As she made her way slowly downhill, clutching at tree-trunks and branches to keep from falling over, two detectives from the attorney general's office were questioning her mother and brother. Later that afternoon a psychiatrist who worked with the state police would try to hypnotize them, and with Pete he would succeed. The focus of their questions had to do with pulling into the parking lot on Saturday morning and getting ready to hike. Had they seen a blue van? Had they seen a man with blond hair and eyeglasses?

'Dear Christ,' Quilla said, finally giving in to the tears she had until now largely held off. 'Dear Christ, you think my baby was kidnapped, don't you? Snatched from behind us while we were arguing.' At that, Pete also began to cry.

In TR-90, TR-100, and TR-110, the search for Trisha went on, but the perimeter had been tightened, the men and women in the woods instructed to concentrate more fully on the area near where the girl had last been seen. The searchers were now looking more for the girl's effects than for the girl herself: her pack, her poncho, articles of her clothing. Not her panties, though; the A.G.'s men and the state police detectives were pretty sure no one would find those. Guys like Mazzerole usually kept their victims' undergarments, holding onto them long after the bodies had been tossed in ditches or stuffed into culverts.

Trisha McFarland, who had never seen Francis Raymond

Mazzerole in her life, was now thirty miles beyond the northwest perimeter of the new, tighter search area. The Maine State Guides and Forest Services game wardens would have found this difficult to believe even without the false tip to distract them, but it was true. She was no longer in Maine; at around three o'clock that Monday afternoon she crossed over into New Hampshire.

It was an hour or so after that when Trisha saw the bushes near a stand of beech trees not far from the stream. She walked toward them, not daring to believe even when she saw the bright red berries – hadn't she just told herself that she could see things and hear them if she wanted to badly enough?

True . . . but she'd also told herself that if she was surprised, the things she saw and heard might be real. Another four steps convinced her that the bushes *were* real. The bushes . . . and the lush freight of checkerberries hanging all over them like tiny apples.

'Berries ho!' she cried in a cracked, hoarse voice, and any last doubts were removed when two crows which had been feasting on dropped fruit a little farther into the tangle took wing, cawing at her reprovingly.

Trisha meant to walk, but found herself running instead. When she reached the bushes she stopped on her heels, breathing hard, her cheeks flushed in thin lines of color. She reached out with her filthy hands, then pulled them back, still convinced on some level that when she tried to touch, her fingers would go right through. The bushes would shimmer like a special effect in a movie (one of Pete's beloved 'morphs'), and then they would show them-selves for what they really were: just more tangles of cruddy brown brambles, ready to drink as much of her blood as they could while it was still warm and flowing.

'*No,*' she said, and reached forward. For a moment she still wasn't sure, and then . . . oh, and then—

The checkerberries were small and soft under her fingertips. She squashed the first one she picked; it spurted droplets of red juice onto her skin and made her think of once when she had been watching her father shave and he had nicked himself.

She raised the finger with the droplets on it (and a little scrap of deflated berry-skin) to her mouth and put it between her lips. The taste was tangy-sweet, reminding her not of Teaberry gum but of Cranapple juice, just poured from a bottle kept cold in the refrigerator. The taste made her cry, but she wasn't aware of the tears spilling down her cheeks. She was already reaching for more berries, stripping them from the leaves in sticky bleeding bunches, cramming them into her mouth, hardly chewing, simply swallowing them and groping for more.

Her body opened itself to the berries; basked in their sugary arrival. She felt this happen – was totally *down* with it, as Pepsi might have said. Her thinking self seemed far away, watching it all. She harvested the berries from their branches, closing her hand around whole clumps of them and pulling them off. Her fingers turned red; her palms; so, in very short order, did her mouth. As she pushed deeper into the bushes, she began to look like a girl who had been in a nasty cutting-scrape and needed a quick patch-up in the nearest emergency room.

She ate some of the leaves as well as the berries, and her mother had been right about them, too – they were good even if you *weren't* a woodchuck. Zippy. The two tastes combined made her think of the jelly Gramma McFarland served with roast chicken.

She might have gone on eating her way south for quite awhile longer, but the berry-patch came to an abrupt end. Trisha emerged from the last clump of bushes and found herself looking into the mild, startled face and dark brown eyes of a good-sized doe. She dropped a double handful of berries and screamed through what now looked like a crazy application of lipstick.

The doe hadn't been bothered by her crackling, munching progress through the checkerberry tangle, and seemed just mildly annoyed by Trisha's scream – it occurred to Trisha later that this was one deer who would be lucky to survive hunting season come fall. The doe merely flicked her ears and took two springy steps – they were more like bounces, actually – back into a clearing which was shafted by conflicting rays of dusky green-gold light.

Beyond her, watching more warily, were two fawns on gangly legs. The doe took another look over her shoulder at Trisha, then crossed with those light, springing steps to her kids. Watching her, amazed and as delighted as she had been at the sight of the beavers, Trisha thought that the doe moved like a creature with a thin coating of that Flubber stuff on her feet.

The three deer stood in the beech clearing, almost as if posing for a family portrait. Then the doe nudged one of the fawns (or perhaps bit its flank), and the three of them were on their way. Trisha saw the flirt of their white tails going downhill and then she had the clearing to herself.

'Goodbye!' she called. 'Thanks for stopping b—'

She stopped, realizing what the deer had been doing here. The forest floor was littered with beechnuts. She knew about these not from her mother but from science class at school. Fifteen minutes ago she had been starving; now she was in the middle of Thanksgiving dinner . . . the vegetarian version, yeah, but so what?

Trisha knelt, picked up one of the nuts, and set the remains of her fingernails in the shell's seam. She didn't expect much, but it opened almost as easily as a peanut. The shell was the size of a knuckle, the nutmeat a little bigger than a sunflower seed. She tried it, a bit dubious, but it was good. In its own way it was as good as the checkerberries, and her body seemed to want it in a different way.

The worst of her hunger had been satisfied by the berries; she had no idea how many she had already gobbled (not to mention the leaves; her teeth were probably as green as Arthur Rhodes's, that creepy little kid who lived up the street from Pepsi). Besides, her stomach had probably shrunk. What she had to do now was . . .

'Stock up,' she muttered. 'Yeah, baby, stock up bigtime.'

She unshouldered her pack, aware of how radically her energy level had rebounded already – it was beyond amazing, actually a little eerie – and unbuckled the flap. She crawled across the clearing, gathering nuts with dirty hands. Her hair hung in her eyes, her filthy shirt flapped, and every now and again she hitched at her jeans, which had been all right when she put them on a thousand years ago but no longer wanted to stay up. As she gathered she sang the auto-glass jingle – 1-800-54-GIANT – under her breath. When she had enough beechnuts to weight down the bottom of the pack, she worked her way slowly back through the checkerberry patch, picking berries and dumping them (the ones she didn't just dump into her mouth) in on top of the nuts.

When she reached the place where she had stood earlier, trying to muster up enough courage to reach out and touch what she saw, she felt almost herself again. Not entirely, but still pretty good. *Whole* was the word that occurred to her, and she liked it so well she said it out loud, not once but twice.

She trudged to the brook, dragging the pack beside her, then sat down under a tree. In the water, like a happy omen, she saw a small speckled fish shoot by in the direction of the flow: a baby trout, perhaps.

Trisha sat where she was for a moment, turning her face up to the sun and closing her eyes. Then she dragged her pack into her lap and put her hand inside, mixing the berries and nuts together. Doing this made her think of Uncle Scrooge McDuck playing around in his money-vault, and she laughed delightedly. The image was absurd and perfect at the same time.

She hulled a dozen or so of the beechnuts, mixed them with a like number of berries (this time using her madder-stained fingers to remove the stems with ladylike care), and tossed the result into her mouth in three measured hand-fuls: dessert. The taste was heavenly – like one of those trailmix breakfast cereals her mother always ate – and when Trisha had finished the last handful, she realized she wasn't just full but gorged. She didn't know how long the feeling would last – probably nuts and berries were like Chinese food, they filled you up and an hour later you were hungry again – but right now her midsection felt like an over-loaded Christmas stocking. It was wonderful to be full. She had lived nine years without knowing that, and she hoped she would never forget: it was wonderful to be full.

Trisha leaned back against the tree and looked into her knapsack with deep happiness and gratitude. If she hadn't been so full (*too stuffed to jump,* she thought), she would have stuck her head in like a mare sticking her head into an oatsack, just to fill her nose with the delicious combined smell of the checkerberries and beechnuts.

'Saved my life, you guys,' she said. 'Saved my goshdarn life.'

On the far side of the rushing stream there was a little clearing carpeted with pine needles. Sunlight fell into it in bright yellow bars filled with slow-dancing pollen and woods dust. Butterflies also played in this light, dipping and swooping. Trisha crossed her hands on her belly, where the roaring was now still, and watched the butterflies. In that moment she did not miss her mother, father, brother, or best friend. In that moment she did not even want to go home, although she ached all over and her butt stung and itched and chafed when she walked. In that moment she was at peace, and more than at peace. She was experiencing her life's greatest contentment. *If I get out of this I'll never be able to tell them,* she thought. She watched the butter-flies on the other side of the stream, her eyelids drooping. There were two white ones; the third was velvety-dark, brown or maybe black.

Tell them what, sugar? It was the tough tootsie, but for once she didn't sound cold, only curious.

What there really is. How simple. Just to eat . . . why, just to have something to eat and then to be full afterward . . .

'The Subaudible,' Trisha said. She watched the butter-flies. Two white and one dark, all three dipping and darting in the afternoon sun. She thought of Little Black Sambo up in the tree, the tigers running around down below and wearing his fine new clothes, running and running until they melted and turned into butter. Into what her Dad called ghee.

Her right hand came unlaced from her left, rolled over, and thumped palm-up to the ground. It seemed like too much work to put it back and so Trisha let it stay where it was.

The Subaudible what, sugar? What about it?

'Well,' Trisha said in a slow, sleepy, considering voice. 'It's not like that's *nothing* . . . is it?'

The tough tootsie didn't reply. Trisha was glad. She felt so sleepy, so full, so wonderful. She didn't sleep, though; even later, when she knew she must have slept, it didn't seem as if she had. She remembered thinking about her Dad's back yard behind the newer, smaller house, how the grass needed cutting and the lawn-dwarves looked sly – as if they knew something you didn't – and about how Dad had started to look sad and old to her, with that smell of beer always coming out of his pores. Life could be very sad, it seemed to her, and mostly it was what it could be. People made believe that it wasn't, and they lied to their kids (no movie or television program she had ever seen had prepared her for losing her balance and plopping back into her own crap, for instance) so as not to scare them or bum them out, but yeah, it could be sad. The world had teeth and it could bite you with them anytime it wanted.

She knew that now. She was only nine, but she knew it, and she thought she could accept it. She was almost ten, after all, and big for her age.

I don't know why we have to pay for what you guys did wrong! That was the last thing she had heard Pete say, and now Trisha thought she knew the answer. It was a tough answer but probably a true one: just because. And if you didn't like it, take a ticket and get in line.

Trisha guessed that in a lot of ways she was older than Pete now.

She looked downstream and saw that another stream came pouring into hers about forty yards from where she was sitting; it came over the bank in a spraying little water-fall. Good deal. This was the way it was supposed to work. This second stream she had found *would* get bigger and bigger, this one *would* lead her to people. It—

She shifted her eyes back to the little clearing on the other side of the stream and three people were standing there, looking at her. At least she assumed they were looking at her; Trisha couldn't see their faces. Their feet, either. They wore long robes like the priests in those movies about days of old. ('In days of *old* when knights were *bold* and ladies showed their *fan*-nies,' Pepsi Robichaud sometimes sang when she jumped rope.) The hems of these robes puddled on the clearing's carpet of needles. Their hoods were up, hiding the faces within. Trisha looked across the stream at them, a little startled but not really afraid, not then. Two of the robes were white. The one worn by the figure in the middle was black.

'Who are you?' Trisha asked. She tried to sit up a little straighter and found she couldn't. She was too full of food.

For the first time in her life she felt as if she had been *drugged* with food. 'Will you help me? I'm lost. I've been lost for . . .' She couldn't remember. Was it two days or three? '. . . for a long time. Will you please help me?'

They didn't answer, only stood there looking at her (she *assumed* they were looking at her, anyway), and that was when Trisha began to feel afraid. They had their arms crossed on their chests and you couldn't even see their hands, because the long sleeves of their robes flowed over them.

'Who are you? Tell me who you are!'

The one on the left stepped forward, and when he reached up to his hood his white sleeves fell away from long white fingers. He pushed the hood back and revealed an intelligent (if rather horsey) face with a receding chin. He looked like Mr. Bork, the science teacher at Sanford Elementary who had taught them about the plants and animals of northern New England . . . including, of course, the world-famous beechnut. Most of the boys and some of the girls (Pepsi Robichaud, for instance) called him Bork the Dork. He looked at her from across the stream and from behind little gold-rimmed spectacles.

'I come from the God of Tom Gordon,' he said. 'The one he points up to when he gets the save.'

'Yes?' Trisha asked politely. She wasn't sure she trusted this guy. If he'd said he *was* the God of Tom Gordon, she knew damned well she wouldn't have trusted him. She could believe a lot of things, but not that God looked like her fourth-grade science teacher. 'That's . . . very interesting.'

'He can't help you,' Bork the Dork said. 'There's a lot going on today. There's been an earthquake in Japan, for instance, a bad one. As a rule he doesn't intervene in human affairs, anyway, although I must admit he *is* a sports fan. Not necessarily a Red Sox fan, however.'

He stepped back and raised his hood. After a moment the other whiterobe, the one on the right, stepped forward . . . as Trisha had known he would. These things had a certain form to them, after all – three wishes, three trips up the beanstalk, three sisters, three chances to guess the evil dwarf's name. Not to mention three deer in the woods, eating beechnuts.

Am I dreaming? she asked herself, and reached up to touch the wasp-sting on her left cheekbone. It was there, and although the swelling had gone down some, touching it still hurt. Not a dream. But when the second whiterobe pushed back his hood and she saw a man who looked like her father – not exactly, but as much like Larry McFarland as the first whiterobe had looked like Mr. Bork – she thought it had to be. If so, it was like no other dream she had ever had.

'Don't tell me,' Trisha said, 'you come from the Subaudible, right?'

'Actually, I *am* the Subaudible,' the man who looked like her father said apologetically. 'I had to take the shape of someone you know in order to appear, because I'm actually quite weak. I can't do anything for you, Trisha. Sorry.'

'Are you drunk?' Trisha asked, suddenly angry. 'You are, aren't you? I can smell it from here. Boy!'

The Subaudible guy gave her a shamefaced little smile, said nothing, stepped back, raised his hood.

Now the figure in the black robe stepped forward. Trisha felt sudden terror.

'No,' she said. 'Not you.' She tried to get up and still couldn't move. 'Not you, go away, give me a break.'

But the black-clad arms rose, falling away from yellow-white claws . . . the claws that had left the marks on the trees, the claws that had torn off the deer's head and then ripped its body apart.

'No,' Trisha whispered. 'No, don't, please. I don't want to see.'

The blackrobe paid no attention. It pushed back its hood. There was no face there, only a misshapen head made of wasps. They crawled over each other, jostling and buzzing. As they moved Trisha saw disturbing ripples of human feature: an empty eye, a smiling mouth. The head hummed as the flies had hummed on the deer's ragged neck; it hummed as though the creature in the black robe had a motor for a brain.

'I come from the thing in the woods,' the blackrobe said in a buzzing, inhuman voice. He sounded to Trisha like that guy on the radio who told you not to smoke, the one who had lost his vocal cords in a cancer operation and had to talk through a gadget he held to his throat. 'I come from the God of the Lost. It has been watching you. It has been waiting for you. It is your miracle, and you are its.'

'Go away!' Trisha tried to yell this, but only a husky whining whisper actually came out.

'The world is a worst-case scenario and I'm afraid all you sense is true,' said the buzzing wasp-voice. Its claws raked slowly down the side of its head, goring through its insect flesh and revealing the shining bone beneath. 'The skin of the world is woven of stingers, a fact you have now learned for yourself. Beneath there is nothing but bone and the God we share. This is persuasive, do you agree?'

Terrified, crying, Trisha looked away – looked back down the stream. She found that when she wasn't looking at the hideous wasp-priest, she could move a little. She raised her hands to her cheeks, wiped away her tears, then looked back. 'I don't believe you! I don't—'

The wasp-priest was gone. All of them were gone. There were only butterflies dancing in the air across the stream, eight or nine now instead of just three, all different colors instead of just white and black. And the light was different; it had begun to take on a gold-orange hue. Two hours had gone by at least, probably more like three. So she had slept. 'It was all a dream,' as they said in the stories . . . but she couldn't remember going to sleep no matter how hard she tried, couldn't remember any break in her chain of consciousness at all. And it hadn't *felt* like a dream.

An idea occurred to Trisha then, one which was simultaneously frightening and oddly comforting: perhaps the nuts and berries had gotten her high as well as feeding her. She knew there were mushrooms that could get you high, that sometimes kids ate pieces of them to get off, and if mushrooms could do that, why not checkerberries? 'Or the leaves,' she said. 'Maybe it was the leaves. I bet it was.' Okay, no more of *them*, zippy or not.

Trisha got up, grimaced as a cramp pulled at her belly, and bent over. She passed gas and felt better. Then she went to the stream, spotted a couple of good-sized rocks sticking out of the water, and used them to hop across. In some ways she felt like a different girl, clear-eyed and full of energy, yet the thought of the wasp-priest haunted her, and she knew her unease would only get worse after the sun went down.

If she wasn't careful, she'd have the horrors. But if she could prove to herself it had only been a dream, brought on by eating checkerberry leaves or maybe by drinking water that her system still wasn't entirely used to . . .

Actually being in the small clearing made her feel nervous, like a character in a slasher movie, the stupid girl who goes into the psycho's house asking, 'Is anybody here?' She looked back across the stream, immediately felt that something was looking at her from the woods on this side, and reversed direction so fast she almost fell down. Nothing there. Nothing anywhere, as far as she could tell.

'You dingbat,' she said softly, but that feeling of being watched had come back, and come back strong. The God of the Lost, the wasp-priest had said. It has been watching you, it has been waiting for you. The wasp-priest had said other things, too, but that was what she remembered: *Watching you, waiting for you.*

Trisha went to where she was pretty sure she had seen the three robed figures and looked for any sign of them, any sign at all. There was nothing. She dropped to one knee to look more closely and there was still nothing, not so much as a patch of scuffed needles which her frightened mind could have interpreted as a footprint. She got up again, turned to cross the stream, and as she did, something in the forest to her right caught her eye.

She walked in that direction, then stood looking into the tangled darkness where young trees with thin trunks grew close together, fighting for space and light aboveground, no doubt fighting with the grasping bushes for moisture and root-room below. Here and there in the darkening green, birches stood like gaunt ghosts. Splashed across the bark of one of these was a stain. Trisha looked nervously over her shoulder, then pushed her way into the woods and toward the birch. Her heart was thumping hard in her chest and her mind was screaming at her to stop this, to not be such a fool, such a dingbat, such an *asshole,* but she went on.

Lying at the foot of the birch was a snarly coil of bleeding intestine so fresh that it had as yet collected only a few flies. Yesterday the sight of such a thing had had her struggling with all her might not to throw up, but life seemed different today; things had changed. There were no butterflutters, no meaty hiccups way down deep in her throat, no instinctive urge to turn away or at least avert her eyes. Instead of these things she felt a coldness that was somehow much worse. It was like drowning, only from the inside out.

There was a swatch of brown fur caught in the bushes to one side of the guts, and on it she could see a spatter of white spots. This was the remains of a fawn, one of the two she had come upon in the beechnut clearing, she was quite sure. Further into the trees, where the woods were already darkening toward night, she saw an alder tree with more of those deep claw-marks slashed into it. They were high up, where only a very tall man could have reached. Not that Trisha believed a man had made the marks.

It has been watching you. Yes, and was watching again right now. She could feel eyes crawling on her skin the way the little bugs, the minges and noseeums, crawled there. She might have dreamed the three priests, or hallucinated them, but she wasn't hallucinating the deerguts or the claw-marks on the alder. She wasn't hallucinating the feel of those eyes, either.

Breathing hard, her own eyes jerking from side to side

in their sockets, Trisha backed toward the sound of the stream, expecting to see *it* in the woods, the God of the Lost. She broke free of the underbrush and, clutching small branches, backed all the way to the stream. When she was there, she whirled and leaped across it on the rocks, partly convinced that even now *it* was bursting out of the woods behind her, all fangs, claws, and stingers. She slipped on the second rock, almost fell into the water, managed to keep her balance, and staggered up on the far bank. She turned and looked back. Nothing over there. Even most of the butterflies were gone now, although one or two still danced, reluctant to give up the day.

This would probably be a good place to spend the night, close to the checkerberry bushes and the beechnut clearing, but she couldn't stay where she had seen the priests. They were probably just figures in a dream, but the one in the black robe had been horrible. Also, there was the fawn. Once the flies *did* arrive in force, she would hear them buzzing.

Trisha opened her pack, got a handful of berries, then paused. 'Thank you,' she told them. 'You're the best food I ever ate, you know.'

She set off downstream again, hulling and munching a few beechnuts as she went. After a little bit she began to sing, at first tentatively and then with surprising enthusiasm as the day waned: 'Put your arms around me . . . cuz I gotta get next to you . . . all your love forever . . . you make me feel brand new . . .'

Yeah, baby.

TOP OF THE SEVENTH

As twilight thickened toward true dark, Trisha came to a rocky open place that looked out over a small, blue-shadowed valley. She surveyed this valley eagerly, hoping to see lights, but there were none. A loon cried from somewhere and a crow called crossly back. That was all.

She looked around and saw several low rock outcrops with drifts of pine needles lying between them like hammocks. Trisha put her pack down at the head of one of these, went to the nearest stand of pine, and broke off enough boughs to make a mattress. It would hardly be a Serta Perfect Sleeper, but she thought it would do. The coming dark had brought on now-familiar feelings of loneliness and sorrowful homesickness, but the worst of her terror was gone. Her sense of being watched had slipped away. If there really was a thing in the woods, it had gone off and left her to herself again.

Trisha went back to the stream, knelt, drank. She had had little stomach-cramps off and on all day, but she thought her body was adapting to the water, nevertheless. 'No problem with the nuts and berries, either,' she said, then smiled. 'Except for a few bad dreams and such.'

She went back to her pack and her makeshift bed, got her Walkman, and settled the earbuds into place. A breeze puffed by her, cold enough to chill her sweaty skin and make her shiver. Trisha dug out the ruins of her poncho and fluffed the dirty blue plastic over her like a blanket. Not much in the way of warmth, but (this was one of Mom's) it's the thought that counts.

She pushed the power button on the Walkman, but although she hadn't changed the tuner's setting, tonight she got nothing but wavers of faint static. She had lost WCAS.

Trisha worked her way across the FM dial. She got faint classical music up around 95 and a Bible-thumper yelling about salvation at 99. Trisha was very interested in salvation, but not the kind the guy on the radio was talking about; the only help from the Lord she wanted right now was a helicopter filled with friendly waving people. She tuned further, got Celine Dion loud and clear at 104, hesitated, then kept on rolling the tuner. She wanted the Red Sox tonight – Joe and Troop, not Celine singing about how her heart would go on and on.

No baseball on the FM, in fact nothing else at all. Trisha switched to the AM band and tuned up toward 850, which was WEEI in Boston. 'EEI was the Red Sox flagship station. She didn't expect perfect reception or anything, but she was hopeful; you could pick up a lot of AM at night, and 'EEI had a strong signal. It would probably waver in and out, but she could put up with that. She didn't have a lot else to do tonight, no hot dates or anything.

'EEI's reception was good – clear as a bell, in fact – but Joe and Troop weren't on. In their place was one of the guys her Dad called 'talk-show idiots.' This one was a *sports* talk-show idiot. Could it be raining in Boston? Game canceled, empty seats, tarp on the field? Trisha looked doubt-fully up at her piece of the sky, where the first stars were now shining like sequins on dark blue velvet. There would be a zillion of them before long; she couldn't see so much as a single cloud. Of course she was a hundred and fifty miles from Boston, maybe more, but—

The talk-show idiot was on the line with Walt from Framingham. Walt was on his car phone. When the talk-show idiot asked where he was now, Walt from Framingham said, 'Somewhere in Danvers, Mike,' pronouncing the town's name as Massachusetts people all did – *Danvizz,* making it sound not like a town but something you'd drink to settle an upset tummy. *Lost in the woods? Been drinking straight from the stream and shitting your brains out as a result? A tablespoon of Danvizz and you'll feel better fast!*

Walt from Framingham wanted to know why Tom Gordon always pointed to the sky when he got a save ('You know, Mike, that pointin thing' was how Walt put it), and Mike the talk-show sports idiot explained it was Number 36's way of thanking God.

'He ought to point to Joe Kerrigan instead,' Walt from Framingham said. 'It was Kerrigan's idea to turn him into a closer. As a starter he was for the birds, you know?'

'Maybe God gave Kerrigan the idea, did you ever think of that, Walt?' the talk-show idiot asked. 'Joe Kerrigan being the Red Sox pitching coach, for those of you who might not know.'

'I *do* know, numbwit,' Trisha murmured impatiently.

'We're mostly talking Sox tonight while the Sox enjoy a rare night off,' said Mike the talk-show idiot. 'They open a three-game set with Oakland tomorrow – yes, West Coast here we come and you'll hear all the action here on WEEI – but today is an open date.'

151

An open date, that explained it. Trisha felt an absurdly huge disappointment weigh her down, and more tears (in Danvizz you called them tizz) began to form in her eyes. She cried so easily now, now she cried over anything. But she had been looking forward to the game, dammit; hadn't known how much she needed the voices of Joe Castiglione and Jerry Trupiano until she found out she wouldn't be hearing them.

'We've got some open lines,' the talk-show idiot said, 'let's fill em up. Anybody out there think Mo Vaughn ought to stop acting like a kid and just sign on the dotted line? How much Mo' money does this guy need, anyway? Good question, isn't it?'

'It's a *stupid* question, El Dopo,' Trisha said pettishly. 'If you could hit like Mo, you'd ask for a lot of money, too.'

'Want to talk about Marvelous Pedro Martinez? Darren Lewis? The surprising Sox bullpen? A *nice* surprise from the Red Sox, can you believe it? Give me a call, tell me what you think. Back after this.'

A happy voice began singing a familiar jingle: 'Who do you call when your *wind*shield's *bus*ted?'

'1-800-54-GIANT,' Trisha said, and then dialed away from 'EEI. Maybe she could find another game. Even the hated Yankees would do. But before she found any baseball, she was transfixed by the sound of her own name.

'— is fading for nine-year-old Patricia McFarland, missing since Saturday morning.'

The news announcer's voice was faint, wavery, sliced and diced by static. Trisha leaned forward, her fingers going to her ears and pressing the little black buds deeper in.

'Connecticut law enforcement authorities, acting on a

tip phoned in to state police in Maine, today arrested Francis Raymond Mazzerole of Weymouth, Massachusetts, and questioned him for six hours in connection with the McFarland girl's disappearance. Mazzerole, a construction worker currently employed on a Hartford bridge project, has twice been convicted of child molestation, and is being held pending extradition to Maine on current charges of sexual assault and child molestation there. It now seems that he has no knowledge of Patricia McFarland's whereabouts, however. A source close to the investigation says that Mazzerole claims to have been in Hartford over the past weekend, and that numerous witnesses corroborate . . .'

The sound faded out. Trisha pushed the power button and pulled the earbuds out of her ears. Were they still looking for her? They probably were, but she had an idea that they'd spent most of today hanging around that guy Mazzerole instead.

'What a bunch of El Dopos,' she said disconsolately, and returned her Walkman to her pack. She lay back on the pine boughs, spread her poncho over her, then shuffled her shoulders and butt around until she was close to comfortable. A breeze puffed past, and she was glad she was in one of the hammocky dips between the rock outcrops. It was chilly tonight, and would probably be downright cold before the sun came up.

Overhead in the black were a zillion stars, just as forecast. Exactly one zillion. They would pale a bit when the moon rose, but for now they were bright enough to paint her dirty cheeks with frost. As always, Trisha wondered if any of those brilliant specks were warming other live beings. Were there jungles out there populated by fabulous alien animals? Pyramids? Kings and giants? Possibly even some version of baseball?

'Who do you call when your *wind*shield's *bus*ted?' Trisha sang softly. '1-800-54—'

She broke off, drawing swift breath in over her lower lip, as if hurt. White fire scratched the sky as one of the stars fell. The streak ran halfway across the black and then winked out. Not a star, of course, not a real star but a meteor.

There was another, and then another. Trisha sat up, the split rags of her poncho falling into her lap, her eyes wide. Here was a fourth and fifth, these going in a different direction. Not just a meteor but a meteor *shower*.

As if something had only been waiting for her to understand this, the sky lit up in a silent storm of bright contrails. Trisha stared, neck tilted, eyes wide, arms crossed over her breastless chest, hands clutching her shoulders with nervous nail-bitten fingers. She had never seen anything like it, never dreamed there *could* be anything like it.

'Oh, Tom,' she whispered in a trembling voice. 'Oh Tom, look at this. Do you see?'

Most were momentary white flashes, thin and straight and gone so quickly that they would have seemed like hallucinations if there hadn't been so many of them. A few, however – five, perhaps eight – lit up the sky like silent fireworks, brilliant stripes that seemed to burn orange at the edges. That orange might just have been eye-dazzle, but Trisha didn't think so.

At last the shower began to wane. Trisha lay back again and scooted the various sore parts of her body around some more until she was comfortable again . . . as comfortable as she was apt to get, anyway. As she did, she watched the ever more occasional flashes as bits of rock further off the path than she could ever get dropped into earth's well of gravity, first turning red as the atmosphere thickened and then burning to death in brief glares of light. Trisha was still watching when she fell asleep.

Her dreams were vivid but fragmentary: a kind of mental meteor shower. The only one she remembered with any clarity was the one she had been having just before she woke up in the middle of the night, coughing and cold, lying on her side with her knees drawn all the way up to her chin and shivering all over.

In this dream she and Tom Gordon were in an old meadow which was now running to bushes and young trees, mostly birches. Tom was standing by a splintery post that came up to about the height of his hip. On top of it was an old ringbolt, rusty red. Tom was flicking this back and forth between his fingers. He was wearing his warmup jacket over his uniform. The gray road uniform. He would be in Oakland tonight. She had asked Tom about 'that pointin thing.' She knew, of course, but asked anyway. Possibly because Walt from Framingham had wanted to know, and a cellular El Dopo like Walt wouldn't believe any little girl lost in the woods; Walt would want it straight from the closer's mouth.

'I point because it's God's nature to come on in the bottom of the ninth,' Tom said. He spun the ringbolt on top of the post back and forth between his fingers. Back and forth, back and forth. Who do you call when your ringbolt's busted? Dial 1-800-54-RINGBOLT, of course. 'Especially when the bases are loaded and there's only one out.' Something in the woods chattered at that, perhaps in derision. The chattering grew louder and louder until Trisha opened her eyes in the dark and realized it was the sound of her own teeth.

She got slowly to her feet, wincing as every part of her body protested. Her legs were the worst, closely followed by her back. A gust of wind struck her – not a puff this time but a gust – and almost knocked her over. She wondered how much weight she had lost. *A week of this and you'll be able to put a string around me and fly me like a kite,* she thought. She started to laugh at that, and the laugh turned into another coughing fit. She stood with her hands planted on her legs just above her knees, her head down, coughing. The cough started deep in her chest and came out of her mouth in a series of harsh barks. Great. Just great. She put the inside of her wrist to her forehead and couldn't tell if she had a fever or not.

Walking slowly with her legs spread far apart – her butt chafed less when she did that – Trisha went back to the pines and broke off more branches, this time meaning to pile them on top of her like blankets. She took one armload back to her bed, got a second, and stopped halfway between the trees and the needle-floored dip she'd chosen to sleep in. Slowly, she turned in a complete circle under the blazing four o'clock stars.

'Leave me alone, can't you?' she cried, and that started her coughing again. When she got the cough under control, she said it again, but in a lower voice: 'Can't you quit it? Can't you just cut me a break, let me be?'

Nothing. No sound but the soughing of the wind through the pines . . . and then a grunt. Low and soft and not even remotely human. Trisha stood where she was with her arms around her fragrant, sappy load of branches. Her skin broke out in hard little bumps. Where had that grunt come from? This side of the stream? The other side? From the stand of pines? She had a horrible idea, almost a certainty, that it was the pines. The thing which had been watching her was in the pines. As she harvested branches to cover herself with, its face had been perhaps less than three feet from her own; its claws, the ones which had torn into the trees and ripped both deer apart, had perhaps hovered within inches of her own hands as she bent the branches back and forth, first splintering them and then breaking them.

Trisha started coughing again, and that got her moving. She dropped the branches in a helter-skelter pile and crawled among them without any attempt to create order out of their jumbled chaos. She winced and moaned a little when one of them poked the place on her hip where she had been stung, then lay still. She sensed it coming now, slipping out of the pines and finally coming for her. The tough tootsie's special thing, the wasp-priest's God of the Lost. You could call it whatever you wanted – the lord of dark places, the emperor of understairs, every kid's worst nightmare. Whatever it was, it had finished teasing her; it was all done playing games. It would simply tear away the branches beneath which she was cowering and eat her alive.

Coughing and shivering, all sense of reality and rationality gone – temporarily insane, in fact – Trisha put her arms over the back of her head and waited to be torn open by the thing's claws and stuffed into its fangy mouth.

She fell asleep that way, and when she woke in the early light of Tuesday morning, both of her arms were asleep from the elbows down and at first she couldn't bend her neck at all; she had to walk with her head cocked slightly to one side.

I guess I won't have to ask either Gramma what it's like to be old, she thought as she squatted to pee. *I guess that now I know.*

As she walked back to the pile of branches where she had slept (like a chipmunk in a burrow, she thought wryly), she saw that one of the other needle-filled hammocks — the one nearest hers, in fact — looked disturbed. The needles had been sprayed around and dug right down to the thin black earth in one place. So maybe she hadn't been insane in the dark of early morning, after all. Or not *entirely* insane. Because later on, after she'd gone back to sleep, something had come. It had been right next to her, perhaps squatting and watching her sleep. Wondering if it should take her now and finally deciding not to, deciding to let her ripen for at least one more day. To let her sweeten like a checker-berry.

Trisha turned in a circle, feeling a dim sense of déjà vu but not remembering she had turned exactly the same circle in almost exactly the same place only a few hours ago. She stopped when she came back to where she had started, coughing nervously into her hand. The cough made her chest hurt, a small dull pain that was very deep inside. She didn't exactly mind — the pain was warm, at least, and every other part of her felt cold this morning.

'It's gone, Tom,' she said. 'Whatever it is, it's gone again. For a little while, anyway.'

Yes, Tom said, *but it'll be back. And sooner or later you'll have to deal with it.*

'Let the evil of the day be sufficient thereof,' Trisha said. That one was her Gramma McFarland's. She didn't know exactly what it meant but thought she *sort* of knew, and it seemed to fit this occasion.

She sat on a rock beside her hammock and munched three big handfuls of berries and beechnuts, telling herself it was granola. The berries weren't as tasty this morning – a little tough, in fact – and Trisha guessed they would be even less tasty come lunchtime. Still, she made herself eat all three handfuls, then went to the stream for a drink. She saw another of those little trout in it, and although the ones she'd seen so far weren't much bigger than smelts or large sardines, she suddenly decided to try and catch one. The stiffness had begun working out of her body a little, the day was warming as the sun rose, and she had begun to feel a little better. Hopeful, almost. Maybe lucky, too. Even the cough had eased.

Trisha went back to her tangled bed, extracted the remains of her poor old poncho, and spread it on one of the rock outcrops. She hunted for a stone with a sharp edge and found a good one near the place where the stream tumbled over the rounded lip of the bluff and into the valley below. This slope was easily as steep as the one she'd gone sliding down on the day she had gotten lost (that day seemed at least five years ago to Trisha), but she thought it would be a much easier descent. There were lots of trees to hold onto.

Trisha took her improvised cutting tool back to her poncho (spread on the rock like that the poncho looked like a big blue paperdoll) and sawed the hood off below the shoulder-line. She doubted very much if she could actually catch a fish in the hood, but it would be amusing to try and she didn't feel like trying the slope until she had limbered up a little more. She sang softly under her breath as she worked, first the Boyz To Da Maxx song that had been in her head throughout, then the Hansons' 'MMMm-Bop,' then a snatch of 'Take Me Out to the Ballgame.' Mostly, however, she sang the one that went 'Who do you call when your *wind*shield's *bus*ted?'

The chilly breeze of the night before had kept the worst of the bugs away, but as the day heated up the usual cloud of tiny airshow performers coalesced around Trisha's head. She barely noticed them, giving an occasional impatient wave only when they got too close to her eyes.

When she had finished cutting the hood off the poncho she held it upside down, dangling it and studying it with a critical, judicious eye. Interesting. Undoubtedly too stupid to work, but sort of interesting, just the same.

'Who do you call, baby who do you call when the *damn* thing's *bus*ted, oh yeah,' Trisha chanted in a singsongy whisper, and walked over to the stream. She picked out two rocks protruding side by side from the water and planted her feet on them. She gazed down between her spread legs into the rushing current. The stream's pebble-packed bed was wavery but otherwise clear. No fish right now, but so what? If you wanted to be a fishergirl, you had to be patient. 'Put your *arms* around me . . . cause I gotta munch on *you*,' Trisha sang, then laughed. Pretty goofy! Holding the hood upside down by the ragged shoulder-material, she bent and dropped her improvised snare into the stream.

The current pulled the hood back between her legs, but it stayed open, so that was all right. The problem was her position – back bent, butt in the air, head at the level of her waist. She wouldn't be able to hold this pose long, and if she tried to squat on the rocks, her sore, shaky legs would likely betray her and send her tumbling into the stream. A full-body dunk wouldn't help her cough.

When her temples started to thud, Trisha compromised by bending her knees and lifting her upper body a little. This shifted her eyeline upstream, and she saw three quick-silver flashes – they were fish, all right, there was no doubt – coming toward her. If she'd had time to react, Trisha almost certainly would have jerked the hood and caught none of them. As it was, she had time for only a single thought

(*like underwater shooting stars*)

and then the silver glints were zipping between the rocks she was standing on and right beneath her. One of them missed the hood, but the other two swam right into it.

'Booya!' Trisha screamed.

With that cry – it was as much dismay and shock as joy – Trisha bent forward again and grasped the lower edge of the hood. In doing so she almost overbalanced and went into the stream anyway, but she managed to stay up. She lifted the hood, full of water and slopping over the sides, in both hands. It shifted out of shape as she stepped back to the bank and more water slopped out, soaking the left leg of her jeans from hip to knee. One of the little trout went with it, twisting and flipping its tail in the air, then hitting the water and swimming away.

'*SUGARTIT!*' Trisha screamed, but now she was also

laughing. As she worked her way up the bank, still holding the hood in front of her, she began coughing, as well.

When she reached a level place, she looked into the hood, sure she would see nothing – she had lost the other fish, as well, must have, girls didn't catch trout, even baby ones, in the hoods of their ponchos, she just hadn't seen its getaway. But the trout was still there, swimming around like a mollie in a goldfish bowl.

'God, what do I do now?' Trisha asked. This was a genuine prayer, both agonized and bemused.

It was her body that answered, not her spirit. She had seen plenty of cartoons where Wile E. Coyote looked at Roadrunner and saw him turn into Thanksgiving dinner. She had laughed, Pete laughed, even Mom laughed if she was watching. Trisha did not laugh now. Berries and beech-nuts the size of sunflower seeds were all very well, but they weren't enough. Even when you ate them together and told yourself they were granola, they weren't enough. Her body's reaction to the four-inch trout swimming in the blue hood was radically different, not hunger exactly but a kind of clench, a cramp that centered in her belly but actually came from everywhere, an inarticulate cry

(*GIMME THAT*)

which had little to do with her brain. It was a trout, just a little one far below the legal limit, but whatever her eyes saw, her body saw dinner. *Real* dinner.

Trisha had only one clear thought as she took the hood over to the remains of the poncho, which was still spread on the outcrop (a paperdoll without a head now): *I'll do it but I'll never ever talk about it. If they find me rescue me I'll tell them everything except how I fell into my own shit . . . and this.*

She acted with no planning or consideration; her body brushed her mind aside and simply took over. Trisha spilled the contents of the hood onto the needle-covered ground and watched the little fishie flop about, strangling in the air. When it was still she picked it up, put it on the poncho, and slit it up the belly with the stone she'd used to cut off the poncho's hood. A thimbleful of watery, mucusy fluid ran out, more like thin snot than blood. Inside the fish she could see tiny red guts. These Trisha levered out with a grimy thumbnail. Beyond them was a bone. She tried to pull it free and got about half of it. During all this her mind tried to take over only once. *You can't eat the head,* it told her, its reasonable tone not really masking the horror and disgust beneath. *I mean . . . the eyes, Trisha. The eyes!* Then her body brushed it away again, and more roughly this time. *When I want your opinion I'll rattle the bars in your cage,* Pepsi sometimes said.

Trisha picked up the small flayed fish by the tail, carried it back to the stream, and dipped it to get rid of the pine-needles and grime. Then she cocked her head back, opened her mouth, and bit off the trout's top half. Small bones crunched under her teeth; her mind tried to show her the trout's eyes popping out of its head and onto her tongue in little dark dabs of jelly. She got one blurry look at this and then her body banished her mind yet again, this time slapping instead of merely pushing. Mind could come back when mind was needed; imagination could come back when imagination was needed. Right now body was in charge, and body said dinner, it's dinner, it may be morning but dinner is served and this morning we got fresh fish.

The trout's top half went down her throat like a big

swallow of oil with lumps in it. The taste was horrible and also wonderful. It tasted like life. Trisha dangled the trout's dripping lower half in front of her upturned face, pausing only long enough to pull another piece of bone out of it, whispering: 'Dial 1–800–54–FRESH–FISH.'

She ate the rest of the trout, tail and all.

When it was down she stood looking across the stream, wiping her mouth and wondering if she was going to puke it all back up again. She had eaten a raw fish, and although the taste of it was still coating her throat, she could hardly believe it. Her stomach gave a funny little lurch and Trisha thought, *This is it.* Then she burped and her stomach settled again. She took her hand away from her mouth and saw a few fish-scales gleaming on the palm. She wiped them on her jeans with a grimace, then walked back to where her pack lay. She stuffed the remains of her poncho and the severed hood (which had turned out to work pretty well, at least on fish that were young and stupid) into it on top of her food supply, then reshouldered the pack. She felt strong, ashamed of herself, proud of herself, feverish, and a little nutzoid.

I won't talk about it, that's all. I don't have to talk about it and I won't. Even if I get out of here.

'And I deserve to get out,' Trisha said softly. 'Anyone who can eat a raw fish deserves to get out.'

The Japanese do it all the time, said the tough tootsie as Trisha set out once more along the side of the stream.

'So I'll tell *them*,' Trisha said. 'If I ever get over there for a visit I'll tell *them*.'

For once the tough tootsie seemed to have no comeback. Trisha was delighted.

She made her way carefully down the slope and into the valley, where her stream bowled along through a forest of mixed firs and deciduous trees. These were thickly packed, but there was less underbrush and fewer bramble-patches, and for most of the morning Trisha got along well. There was no sense of being watched, and eating the fish had revitalized her strength. She pretended that Tom Gordon was walking with her, and they had a long and interesting conversation, mostly about Trisha. Tom wanted to know all about her, it seemed — her favorite classes at school, why she thought Mr. Hall was mean for giving homework on Fridays, all the ways Debra Gilhooly had of being such a bitch, how she and Pepsi had planned to go trick-or-treating as Spice Girls last Halloween and Mom had said *Pepsi's* Mom could do whatever she wanted, but no nine-year-old girl of *hers* was going out trick-or-treating in a short skirt, high heels, and a cammi top. Tom sympathized completely with Trisha's utter embarrassment.

She was telling him about how she and Pete were planning to get their Dad a custom-made jigsaw puzzle for his birthday from this company in Vermont that made them (or if that was too expensive, they would settle for a Weed Whacker), when she stopped suddenly. Stopped moving. Stopped talking.

She studied the stream for almost a full minute, the corners of her mouth drooping, one hand waving automatically at the cloud of bugs around her head. The underbrush was creeping back in among the trees now; the trees themselves were stuntier, the light brighter. Crickets hummed and sang.

'No,' Trisha said. 'No, huh-uh. No way. Not again.'

The stream's new quietness was what had first distracted her from her fascinating conversation with Tom Gordon (pretend people were such good listeners). The stream no longer babbled and brawled. That was because the speed of its current had slowed. Its bed was weedier than it had been above the valley's floor. It was beginning to spread out.

'If it goes into another swamp, I'll kill myself, Tom.'

An hour later Trisha pushed her way wearily through a snarl of mixed poplars and birches, raised the heel of her hand to her forehead to crush a particularly troublesome mosquito, and then just left it there, hand to brow, the image of every human in history who is exhausted and doesn't know what to do or where to turn.

At some point the stream had spilled over its low banks and drowned a large area of open land, creating a shallow marsh of reeds and cattails. Between the vegetation, the sun glittered on standing water in hot pricks of light. Crickets hummed; frogs croaked; overhead, two hawks cruised on stiff wings; somewhere a crow was laughing. The marsh didn't look nasty, like the bog of hummocks and drowned deadwood she'd waded through, but it stretched for at least a mile (and probably two) before coming to a low, pine-covered ridge.

And the stream, of course, was gone.

Trisha sat down on the ground, started to say something to Tom Gordon, and realized how stupid it was to be pretending when it was clear — and growing clearer with every passing hour — that she was going to die. It didn't matter how much walking she did or how many fish she managed to catch and choke down. She began to cry. She put her face in her hands, sobbing harder and harder.

'I want my *mother*!' she yelled at the indifferent day. The hawks were gone, but over by that wooded ridge the crow was still laughing. 'I want my *mother*, I want my *brother*, I want my *dolly*, I want to go *home*!' The frogs only croaked, reminding her of some story Dad had read her when she was little – a car stuck in the mud and all the frogs croaking *Too deep, too deep*. How that had frightened her.

She cried harder still, and at some point her tears – all these tears, all these *goshdamn tears* – made her angry. She looked up, bugs spinning all around her, the hateful tears still spilling down her mucky face.

'I want my *MOTHER*! I want my *BROTHER*! I want to *get out of here, DO YOU HEAR ME*?' She kicked her legs up and down, kicked them so hard that one of her sneakers flew off. She knew she was doing a full-fledged tantrum now, the first one since she'd been five or six, and didn't care. She threw herself onto her back, pounded her fists, then opened them so she could tear handfuls of grass out of the ground and throw them into the air. '*I WANT TO GET THE HELL OUT OF HERE! Why don't you find me, you stupid puppy-shit assholes? Why don't you find me? I . . . WANT . . . TO GO . . . HOME!*'

She lay looking up at the sky, panting. Her stomach hurt and her throat was sore from screaming, but she felt a little better, as if she had gotten rid of something dangerous. She put an arm over her face and dozed off, still sniffling.

When she woke up, the sun was over the ridge on the far side of the marsh. It was afternoon again. *Tell me, Johnny, what do we have for our contestants? Well, Bob, we have another*

167

afternoon. It's not much of a prize, but I guess it's the best a bunch of puppy-shit assholes like us can do.

Trisha's head swam when she sat up; a squadron of large black moths unfolded their wings and went flying lazily across her field of vision. For a moment she was sure she was going to faint. The feeling passed, but her throat was still sore when she swallowed, and her head felt hot. *Shouldn't have slept in the sun,* she told herself, except sleeping in the sun wasn't the reason she felt this way. The reason was that she was getting sick.

Trisha put on the sneaker she had kicked off doing her stupid tantrum, then ate a handful of berries and drank some stream-water from her bottle. She spied a cluster of fiddleheads growing at the edge of the marsh and ate them, too. They were fading and a lot tougher than they were tasty, but she forced them down. With high tea over, she stood up and looked across the marsh again, this time shading her eyes from the sun. After a moment she shook her head slowly and wearily – the gesture of a woman instead of a child, and an old woman, at that. She could see the ridge clearly and she was sure it was dry over there, but she couldn't face slogging through another quagmire with her Reeboks tied around her neck. Not even if this one was shallower than the other one and not as nasty underfoot; not for all the late spring fiddleheads in the world. Why should she, with no stream to follow? She was as apt to find help – or another stream – in another, easier, direction.

So thinking, Trisha turned fully north, walking along the east side of the marsh that sprawled across most of the valley's floor. She had done a great many things right since becoming lost – more than she ever would have guessed – but this was a bad decision, the worst she'd made since leaving the path in the first place. Had she crossed the marsh and climbed the ridge, she would have found herself looking down at Devlin Pond, on the outskirts of Green Mount, New Hampshire. Devlin was small, but there were cottages on its south end and a camp-road leading out to New Hampshire Route 52.

On a Saturday or Sunday, Trisha would almost certainly have heard the burr of powerboats on the pond as week-enders towed kids on water-skis; after the Fourth of July there would have been powerboats out there on any day of the week, sometimes so many that they had to weave to avoid each other. But this was midweek in early June, there was no one out on Devlin but a couple of fishermen with little twenty-horse putt-putts, and Trisha consequently heard nothing but the birds and the frogs and the bugs. Instead of finding the pond, she turned toward the Canadian border and began walking deeper into the woods. Some four hundred miles ahead was Montreal.

Between it and her, not much.

SEVENTH INNING STRETCH

The year before the separation and divorce, the McFarlands had gone to Florida for a week, during Pete and Trisha's February school vacation. It had been a bad holiday, with the children too often glumly shelling together on the beach while their parents fought in the little beach house they had rented (he drank too much, she spent too much, you promised me you'd, why don't you ever, yatata-yatata-yatata, dahdah-dahdah-dahdah). When they flew back, Trisha somehow got the window seat instead of her brother. The plane had descended toward Logan Airport through layers of overcast, lumbering as carefully as an overweight old lady walking down a sidewalk where there are patches of ice. Trisha had watched, fascinated, with her forehead pressed to the window. They would be in a perfect world of white . . . there would be a flash of the ground or the slate-gray water of Boston Harbor below them . . . more white . . . then another flash of the ground or the water.

The four days which followed her decision to turn north were like that descent: mostly a cloudbank. Some of the memories she *did* have she did not trust; by Tuesday night the boundary between reality and make-believe had begun to disappear. By Saturday morning, after a full week in the woods, it was all but gone. By Saturday morning (not that Trisha recognized it as Saturday when it came; by then she had lost track of the days) Tom Gordon had become her fulltime companion, not pretend but accepted as real. Pepsi Robichaud walked with her for awhile; the two of them sang all their favorite Boyz and Spice Girls duets and then Pepsi walked behind a tree and didn't come out on the other side. Trisha looked behind the tree, saw that Pepsi wasn't there, and understood after several moments of frowning thought that she had never been there at all. Trisha then sat down and cried.

While she was crossing a wide, boulder-strewn clearing, a large black helicopter – the sort of helicopter the sinister government conspiracy guys used in *The X-Files* – came and hovered over Trisha's head. It was soundless except for the faintest pulse of its rotors. She waved to it and screamed for help, and although the guys inside must have seen her, the black helicopter flew away and never returned. She came to an old forest of pines through which the light slanted in ancient dusty beams like sunrays falling through the high windows of a cathedral. This might have been on Thursday. From these trees hung the mutilated corpses of a thousand deer, a slain army of deer crawling with flies and bulging with maggots. Trisha closed her eyes and when she opened them again the rotting deer were gone. She found a stream and followed it for awhile and then it either quit on her or she wandered away from it. Before this happened, however, she looked into it and saw an enormous face on the bottom, drowned but somehow still living, looking up at her and talking soundlessly. She passed a great gray tree like a hollow crooked hand; from within it, a dead voice spoke her name. One night she awoke with something pressing down on her chest and thought the thing in the woods had finally come for her, but when she reached for it there was nothing there and she could breathe again. On several occasions she heard people calling for her, but when she called back there was never any answer.

Amid these clouds of illusion came vivid flashes of reality like glimpses of the ground. She remembered discovering another berry patch, a huge one splashed down the side of a hill, and refilling her pack while she sang, 'Who do you call when your *wind*shield's *bus*ted?' She remembered filling her water-bottle and Surge bottle from a spring. She remembered stumbling over a root and falling to the bottom of a wet little declivity where the most beautiful flowers she had ever seen grew – waxy-white and aromatic, graceful as bells. She had a clear memory of coming upon the headless body of a fox; unlike the army of slain deer hanging from the trees, this corpse didn't go away when she closed her eyes and counted to twenty. She was quite sure she saw a crow hanging upside down from a branch by its feet and cawing at her, and while that was probably impossible, the memory had a quality that many others (the one of the black helicopter, for instance) did not: a texture and a lucidity. She remembered fishing with her hood in the stream where she later saw the long drowned face. There were no trout but she did manage to catch a few taddies. She ate these whole, being careful to make sure they were dead before she did. She was haunted by the idea that they might live in her stomach, and turn into frogs there.

She was sick, she had been right about that, but her body fought the infection in her throat and chest and sinuses with remarkable tenacity. For hours at a time she would feel feverish, hardly in the world at all. The light, even when it was dim and filtered by heavy tree-cover, hurt her eyes, and she talked nonstop – mostly to Tom Gordon but also to her mother, brother, father, Pepsi, and all the teachers she had ever had, right back to Mrs. Garmond in kindergarten. She woke herself up in the night, lying on her side with her knees curled to her chest, shaking with fever and coughing so hard she feared something inside her would rupture. But then, instead of getting worse, the fever would either fade or disappear entirely, and the headaches which accompanied it would lift. She had one night (it was Thursday, although she didn't know it) when she slept right through and woke almost refreshed. If she had coughed during that night, it wasn't hard enough to wake her. She picked up a patch of poison ivy on her left forearm, but Trisha recognized it for what it was and slathered it with mud. It didn't spread.

Her clearest memories were of lying beneath heaps of branches and listening to the Red Sox while the stars glared coldly overhead. They won two out of three in Oakland, with Tom Gordon getting saves in both wins. Mo Vaughn hit two home runs and Troy O'Leary (one very cute baseball player, in Trisha's humble estimation) hit one. The games came through to her on WEEI, and although the reception grew a little worse each night, her batteries held up well. She remembered thinking that if she ever got out of this, she would have to write a fan letter to the Energizer Bunny. She did her part by turning the radio off when she got sleepy. Not once, even on Friday night, when she was wracked with chills and fever and watery bowels, did she go to sleep with the radio on. The radio was her lifeline, the games her life preserver. Without them to look forward to she thought she would simply give up.

The girl who had gone into the woods (almost ten and big for her age) had weighed ninety-seven pounds. The girl who came blundering half-blind up a piney slope and into a brushy clearing seven days later weighed no more than seventy-eight. Her face was swollen with mosquito bites and a large coldsore had bloomed on the left side of her mouth. Her arms were sticks. She hitched constantly at the waist of her loose jeans without realizing it. She was muttering a song under her breath – 'Put your *arms* around me . . . cuz I gotta get next to *you*' – and looked like one of the world's younger heroin addicts. She had been resourceful, she had been lucky with the weather (moderate temperatures, no rain since the day she'd gotten lost), and she had discovered deep and totally unexpected reserves of strength within herself. Now those reserves were almost gone, and in some part of her exhausted mind, Trisha knew it. The girl making her slow, weaving way through the clearing at the top of the slope was nearly finished.

In the world she had left, a desultory remnant of the search went on, but she was nonetheless now presumed dead by most of those looking for her. Her parents had begun to discuss, in a blundering and still unbelieving way, whether they should have a memorial service or wait for the body to be found. And if they decided to wait, how long? Sometimes the bodies of the lost were never found. Pete said little, but he had grown hollow-eyed and silent. He took Moanie Balogna into his room and sat her in the corner where she could look toward his bed. When he saw his mother looking at the doll, he said, 'Don't you touch it. Don't you dare.'

In that world of lights and cars and paved roads she was

dead. In this one – the one that existed off the path, the one where crows sometimes hung upside down from branches – she was close to it. But she kept on truckin. (That one was her father's.) Her course sometimes wavered a bit to the west or the east, but not often and not much. Her ability to keep moving steadily in one direction was nearly as remarkable as her body's refusal to give in completely to the infections in her chest and throat. Not as helpful, however. Her path took her slowly but steadily away from the larger concentrations of towns and villages and deeper into New Hampshire's chimney.

The thing in the woods, whatever it was, kept her company on her journey. Although she dismissed a great deal of what she felt and thought she saw, she never dismissed her sense of what the wasp-priest had called the God of the Lost; never chalked up the clawed trees (or the headless fox, for that matter) to mere hallucination. When she felt that thing (or heard it – several times she had heard breaking branches in the forest as it kept pace with her, and twice she heard its low inhuman grunt), she never questioned the fact of its actual presence. When the feeling left her, she never questioned that the thing was really gone. She and it were tied together now; they would remain so until she died. Trisha didn't think that would be long now. 'Right around the corner,' her mother would have said, except there were no corners in the woods. Bugs and swamps and sudden drop-offs, but no corners. It wasn't fair that she should die after fighting so hard to stay alive, but the unfairness didn't make her so angry now. It took energy to be angry. It took vitality. Trisha was nearly shot of both.

Halfway across this new clearing, which was no different than a dozen others she had passed through, she began to cough. It hurt deep in her chest, made her feel as if there were a great big hook in there. Trisha doubled over, grabbed hold of a jutting stump, and coughed until tears popped out of her eyes and her vision doubled. When the coughing finally tapered off and stopped, she remained bent over at first, waiting for her heart to slow its fearful pounding. Also for those big black butterflies in front of her eyes to fold their wings and go back to wherever they came from. Good thing she'd had this stump to hold onto or she would have fallen over for sure.

Her eyes went to the stump and her thoughts abruptly ceased. The first to come back was *I'm not seeing what I think I'm seeing. It's another make-believe, another hallucination.* She closed her eyes and counted to twenty. When she opened them the black butterflies were gone, but the rest was the same. The stump wasn't a stump. It was a post. On top, screwed into the gray and spongy old wood, was a rusty red ringbolt.

Trisha grasped it, felt the old iron reality of it. She let go and looked at the flecks of rust on her fingers. She grasped it again, flicked it back and forth. That sense of déjà vu swept her as it had when she had turned in a circle, only it was stronger now, and somehow associated with Tom Gordon. What . . . ?

'You dreamed it,' Tom said. He was standing about fifty feet away with his arms folded and his butt leaned up against a maple tree, dressed in his gray road uniform. 'You dreamed we came to this place.'

'I did?'

'Sure, don't you remember? It was the team's off night. The night you listened to Walt.'

'Walt . . . ?' The name was only vaguely familiar, the significance of it totally lost.

'Walt from Framingham. The El Dopo on the cell phone.'

She started to remember. 'And then the stars fell.'

Tom nodded.

Trisha walked slowly around the post, never taking her hand off the ringbolt. She looked carefully at her surroundings and saw that she wasn't in a clearing at all, not really. There was too much grass – the high green grass you saw in fields or meadows. This *was* a meadow, or had been once, a long time ago. If you ignored the birches and the bushes and let your eye see the whole thing, you couldn't mistake it for anything else. It was a meadow. *People* made meadows, just as people planted posts in the ground, posts with ringbolts on them.

Trisha dropped to one knee and ran a hand up and down the post – lightly, mindful of splinters. Halfway around it she discovered a pair of holes and a twisted pring of old metal. She felt below it in the grass, found nothing at first, and dug deeper into the wiry undergrowth. Down there, caught in old hay and timothy, she found something else. Trisha had to use both hands to rip it free. It turned out to be an ancient rusty hinge. She held it up to the sun. A pencil-thin ray fell through one of the screwholes and put a brilliant pinhead of light on one cheek.

'Tom,' she breathed. She looked toward where he had been, leaning back against the maple with his arms crossed, thinking he would be gone again. He wasn't, though, and although he wasn't smiling, she thought she saw a hint of a smile around his eyes and mouth. 'Tom, look!' She held up the hinge.

'It was a gate,' Tom said.

'A gate!' she repeated rapturously. 'A gate!' Something made by humans, in other words. Folk from the magic world of lights and appliances and 6-12 Insect Repellant.

'This is your last chance, you know.'

'What?' She looked at him uneasily.

'It's the late innings now. Don't make a mistake, Trisha.'

'Tom, you—'

But there was no one there. Tom was gone. Not that she had seen him disappear, exactly, because Tom had never been there in the first place. He was only in her imagination.

What's the secret of closing? she had asked him – she couldn't remember exactly when.

Establishing that it's you who's better, Tom had said, her mind perhaps recycling some half-heard comment from a sports show or maybe a postgame interview watched with her father, his arm around her shoulders, her head leaning against him. *It's best to do it right away.*

Your last chance. Late innings. Don't make a mistake.

How can I do that when I don't even know what I'm doing?

To that there was no answer, so Trisha once more walked around the post with her hand on the ringbolt, as slowly and as delicately as a Saxon girl in some ancient courting ritual of the Maypole. The woods which enclosed the overgrown meadow revolved before her sight the way things did when you were on the merry-go-round at Revere Beach or Old Orchard. They looked no different from the miles of woods she'd already been through, and which way?

Which way was the right way? This was a post but not a signpost.

'A post, not a signpost,' she whispered, walking a little faster now. 'How can I know anything from it when it's a post, not a signpost? How can a numbwit like me . . .'

She had an idea then, and dropped back onto her knees. She banged one shin on a rock, started it bleeding, hardly noticed. Maybe it *was* a signpost. Maybe it was.

Because it had been a gatepost.

Trisha found the holes in the post again, the ones where the hinge-screws had gone. She located herself with her feet to those holes, then crawled slowly away from the post on a straight line. One knee forward . . . then the other . . . then the first—

'*Ow!*' she cried, and yanked her hand out of the grass. That had hurt worse than barking her shin. She looked at her palm and saw little beads of blood oozing up through the caked dirt. Trisha leaned forward on her forearms, pushing aside the grass, knowing what had stabbed into her hand, needing to see it just the same.

It was the ragged stump of the other gatepost, broken off about a foot out of the ground, and she'd really been quite lucky not to hurt herself any more than she had; a couple of the splinters sticking up from that post were a good three inches long and looked as sharp as needles. A little beyond the stump, buried in the white and wiry old grass underlying this June's aggressive new green, was the rest of the post.

Last chance. Late innings.

'Yeah, and maybe somebody expects an awful lot from a kid,' she said. She unshouldered her pack, opened it, yanked out the remains of the poncho, and tore off one of the strips. This she knotted around the stump of the broken-off gatepost, coughing nervously as she did it. Sweat ran down her face. Noseeums came to drink it; some drowned; Trisha didn't notice.

She stood up, reshouldering the pack, and stood between the remaining upright post and the blue strip of plastic marking the downed one.

'Here's where the gate was,' she said. 'Right here.' She looked straight ahead, in a northwest direction. Then she about-faced and gazed southeast. 'I don't know why anyone would put a gate here, but I know that you don't bother unless there's a road or a trail or a riding-path or something. I want ...' Her voice trembled toward tears. She stopped, gulped them back, and started again. 'I want to find the path. *Any* path. Where is it? Help me, Tom.'

Number 36 didn't reply. A jay scolded her and something moved in the woods (not *the* thing, just some animal, maybe a deer – she had seen lots of deer over the last three or four days), but that was all. Before her, all around her, was a meadow so old that it could now pass for just another forest clearing unless you looked closely. Beyond this she saw more woods, more clenches of trees she could not name. She saw no path.

This is your last chance, you know.

Trisha turned, walked northwest across the open space to the woods, then looked back to make sure she had held a straight line. She had, and she looked forward again. Branches moved in a light breeze, casting deceptive dapples of light everywhere, creating what was almost a disco-ball effect. She could see an old fallen log and went to it, slipping between the closely packed trees and ducking under the maddening interlacing branches, hoping . . . but it *was* a log, just a log and not another post. She looked further and saw nothing. Heart thumping, breath coming in anxious, phlegmy little bursts, Trisha fought her way back to the clearing and returned to the place where the gate had been. This time she faced southeast and walked slowly once more to the rim of the woods.

'*Well, here we go,*' Troop always said, '*it's the late innings and the Red Sox need base-runners.*'

Woods. Nothing but woods. Not so much as a game-trail – at least not that Trisha could see – let alone a path. She pushed in a little further, still trying not to cry, knowing that very soon she wouldn't be able to help it. Why did the wind have to be blowing? How could you see anything with all those little puppy-shit dots of sunlight spinning around? It was like being in a planetarium, or something.

'What's that?' Tom asked from behind her.

'What?' She didn't bother turning. Tom's appearances no longer seemed especially miraculous to her. 'I don't see anything.'

'To your left. Just a tiny bit.' His finger, pointing over her shoulder.

'That's just an old stump,' she said, but was it? Or was she just afraid to believe it was a—

'I don't believe so,' said Number 36, and of course he had baseball player's eyes. 'I think that's another post, girl.'

Trisha worked her way to it (and it *was* work; the trees were maddeningly thick here, the bushes heavy, the going underfoot littered and treacherous), and yes, it was another post. This one had rusted nips of barbed wire running up the inside like sharp little bowties.

Trisha stood with one hand on its eroded top and looked deeper into the sun-dappled, deceptive woods. She had a dim memory of sitting in her room on a rainy day and working in an activity book Mom had bought her. There was a picture, an incredibly *busy* picture, and in it you were supposed to find ten hidden objects: a pipe, a clown, a diamond ring, stuff like that.

Now she needed to find the path. *Please God help me find the path,* she thought, and closed her eyes. It was the God of Tom Gordon she prayed to, not her father's Subaudible. She wasn't in Malden now, nor in Sanford, and she needed a God that was really there, one you could point to when – if – you got the save. *Please God, please. Help me in the late innings.*

She opened her eyes as wide as she could and looked without looking. Five seconds went by, fifteen seconds, thirty. And all at once it was there. She had no idea what, exactly, she was seeing – perhaps simply a vector where there were fewer trees and a little more clear light, perhaps only a suggestive pattern of shadows all pointing the same way – but she knew what it was: the last remains of a path.

I can stay on it as long as I don't think about it too much, Trisha told herself, beginning to walk. She came to another post, this one leaning at an acute angle; one more winter of frost and freeze, one more spring of thaw and it would fall and be swallowed in the next summer's grass. *If I think about it too much or look too hard, I'll lose it.*

With that in mind, Trisha began following the few remaining posts of those planted by a farmer named Elias

McCorkle in the year 1905; these marked the wood-drag trail he had made as a young man, before the drink got him and he lost his ambition. Trisha went with her eyes wide, never hesitating (to do so would give thought a chance to creep in and likely betray her). Sometimes there would be a stretch where there were no posts, but she did not stop to hunt through the heavy underbrush for their remains; she allowed the light, the shadow-patterns, and her own instinct to guide her. She walked in such steady fashion for the rest of the day, weaving through heavy clumps of trees and high bramble-chokes with her eyes always on the faint trace of the path. She went on for a good seven hours, and just when she was thinking she'd be sleeping again beneath her poncho, huddling there to keep the worst of the bugs at bay, she came to the edge of another clearing. Three posts, leaning drunkenly this way and that, marched to the middle of it. The remains of a second gate still hung from the last of these posts, mostly held up by the thick twining of grass around its lower two crossbars. Beyond it, a pair of fading ruts grown over with grass and daisies headed south, curving back into the forest again. It was an old woods road.

Trisha walked slowly past the gate and to where the road seemed to begin (or finish up; it all depended, she supposed, on which way you were pointing). She stood still a moment, then dropped to her knees and crawled along one of the ruts. As she did it she started crying again. She crawled across the old road's grassy crown, letting the tall grass tickle beneath her chin, and went up the other rut, still on her hands and knees. She crawled like a person who is blind, calling through her tears as she went.

'A road! It's a road! I found a road! Thank You, God! Thank You, God! Thank You for this road!'

Finally she stopped, slipped off her pack, and lay down in the rut. *This was made by wheels,* she thought, and laughed through her tears. After a little while she rolled over and looked at the sky.

EIGHTH INNING

A few minutes later, Trisha got up. She walked along the road another hour, until the dusk was thick around her. Off in the west, for the first time since the day she got lost, she could hear thunder rumbling. She would want to get in under the thickest clump of trees she could find, and if it rained hard enough she would still get wet. In her present mood Trisha hardly cared.

She stopped between the old wheelruts and was beginning to unshoulder her pack when she saw something ahead in the gloom. Something from the world of people; a thing with corners. She resettled her pack-straps and crept toward the right side of the road, peering like a person who has grown nearsighted but is too vain to wear spectacles. In the west, thunder rumbled a little louder.

It was a truck, or the cab of one, rearing out of the matted undergrowth. Its hood was long and nearly buried in woods ivy. One wing of the hood had been flung up, and Trisha could see there was no engine inside; ferns grew where it had been. The cab was dark red with rust, tilted to one side. The windshield was long gone, but there was still a seat inside. Most of its upholstery had rotted away or been chewed away by small animals.

More thunder, and this time she could see lightning

shiver inside the clouds, which were advancing rapidly and eating the first stars as they came.

Trisha broke off a branch, reached through the open space where the crank-out windshield had been, and beat at the seat's stuffing as briskly as she could. The quantity of dust which rose was amazing – it came drifting out through the windshield cavity and window-holes like mist. Even more amazing was the flood of chipmunks that came boiling up from the floorboards, squeaking and fleeing out through the lozenge-shaped rear window.

'Abandon ship!' Trisha cried. 'We've hit an iceberg! Women and chipmunks fi—' She got a lungful of the dust. The resultant coughing fit wracked her until she sat down heavily with her beating-stick in her lap, gasping for a clear breath and half in a faint. She decided she wasn't going to spend the night in the cab of the truck after all. She wasn't afraid of a few leftover chipmunks, not even of snakes (if there were snakes in residence, she guessed the chipmunks would have moved out long since), but she didn't want to spend eight hours breathing dust and coughing herself blue. It would be great to sleep under an actual roof again, but that was too high a price to pay.

Trisha made her way through the bushes beside the truck cab and then a little way into the woods. She sat down under a good-sized spruce, ate some nuts, drank some water. She was getting low on food and drink again, but she was too tired to worry about that tonight. She had found a road, that was the important thing. It was old and unused, but it might take her somewhere. Of course it might also peter out as the streams had, but she wouldn't think about that now. For now she would allow herself to hope the road would take her where the streams had not.

That night was hot and close, the humid edge of New England's short but sometimes fierce summer. Trisha fanned the neck of her grimy shirt against her grimy neck, stuck out her lower lip and blew hair off her forehead, then resettled her hat and lay back against her pack. She thought of digging out her Walkman and decided not to. If she tried listening to a West Coast game tonight, she'd fall asleep for sure and trash whatever was left of the batteries.

She reclined further, turning the pack into a pillow, feeling something which had been so solidly gone that its return seemed miraculous: simple contentment. 'Thanks, God,' she said. In three minutes she was asleep.

She woke up perhaps two hours later, when the first cold drops of a drenching thundershower found their way through the forest's overlacing and landed on her face. Then thunder cracked the world open and she sat up, gasping. The trees were creaking and groaning in a strong wind, almost a gale, and sudden lightning flashed them into stark news-photo relief.

Trisha struggled to her feet, brushing her hair out of her eyes and then cringing as more thunder banged . . . except it was more of a whipcrack than a bang. The storm was almost directly overhead. She would shortly be drenched, trees or no trees. She grabbed up her pack and blundered back toward the dark, tilted hulk of the truck's cab. Three steps and she stopped, gasping in the wet air and then coughing it out, hardly feeling the leaves and small branches that spanked her neck and arms in the gusty wind. Somewhere in the forest a tree fell over with a rending, splintering crack.

It was here, and very close.

The wind changed direction, spattering her with a faceful of rain, and now she could actually smell it – some rank wild odor that made her think of cages at the zoo. Except the thing out there wasn't in a cage.

Trisha began moving toward the truck cab again, holding one hand up before her to ward off whipping branches and the other clapped to the top of her Red Sox cap to keep it on. Thorns tore at her ankles and calves, and when she came out of the sheltering woods to the edge of her road (so she thought of it, as her road), she was instantly drenched.

As she reached the driver's door of the cab, which hung open with vines twisting in and out through its socket of window, lightning flashed again, painting the whole world purple. In its glare Trisha saw something with slumped shoulders standing on the far side of the road, something with black eyes and great cocked ears like horns. Perhaps they *were* horns. It wasn't human; nor did she think it was animal. It was a god. It was *her* god, the wasp-god, standing there in the rain.

'*NO!*' she screamed, diving into the truck, unmindful of the dusty cloud that puffed up around her and the upholstery's rotting, ancient smell. '*NO, GO AWAY! GO AWAY AND LEAVE ME ALONE!*'

Thunder answered. Rain also answered, drumming down on the cab's rusty roof. Trisha hid her head in her arms and rolled over on her side, coughing and shivering. She was still waiting for it to come when she fell asleep again.

This sleep was deep and – as far as she could remember – dreamless. When she awoke, full daylight had returned. It was hot and sunny, the trees seemingly greener than they had been the day before, the grass lusher, the birds twitting away in the depths of the woods more complacently happy. Water rustled and dripped from leaves and branches; when Trisha raised her head and looked out through the tilted glassless rectangle where the old truck's windshield had been, the first thing she saw was sunlight glaring from the surface of a puddle in one of the road's ruts. The glare was so brilliant that she raised a hand to her eyes, squinting. The afterimage hung in front of her even when the real thing was gone: reflected sky, first blue, then a fading green.

The truck's cab had kept her quite dry despite its lack of glass. There was a puddle on the floor around the ancient control pedals and her left arm had gotten wet, but that was pretty much it. If she had coughed in her sleep, it hadn't been hard enough to wake her up. Her throat felt a little raw and her sinuses were plugged, but those things might improve once she got out of the damned dust.

It was here last night. You saw it.

But had she? Had she really?

It came for you, it meant to take you. Then you climbed into the truck and it decided not to, after all. I don't know why, but that's what happened.

Maybe not, though. Maybe the whole thing had just been the sort of dream you could have when you were half-awake and half-asleep at the same time. Something brought on by waking up to a full-fledged thunderstorm, with lightning flashing and the wind blowing a gale. A situation like that, anyone might see stuff.

Trisha grabbed her pack by one slightly frayed strap and wriggled backward through the driver's side doorhole, raising more dust and trying not to breathe it in. When she was out, she stepped away (still wet, the cab's rusty-red surface had darkened to the color of plums) and started to put her pack on. Then she stopped. The day was bright and warm, the rain was over, she had a road to follow . . . but all at once she felt old and tired and zero at the bone. People could imagine things when they woke up suddenly, especially when they woke up at the height of a thunderstorm. Of course they could. But she wasn't imagining what she was seeing now.

While she slept something had dug a circle through the leaves and needles and underbrush surrounding the abandoned truck cab. It was perfectly clear in the morning light, a curving line of wet black earth in the greenery. Bushes and small trees which had been in the way had been torn out by the roots and thrown aside in broken pieces. The God of the Lost had come and drawn a circle around her as if to say, *Stay clear — she is mine, she is my property.*

TOP OF THE NINTH

Trisha walked all that Sunday with the low, hazy sky beating down on her. In the morning the wet woods steamed, but by early afternoon they were dry again. The heat was immense. She was still glad of the road, but now she wished for shade, as well. She felt feverish again, and not just tired but outright exhausted. The thing was watching her, pacing her through the woods and watching her. The feeling didn't leave her this time because the thing didn't leave her. It was in the woods to her right. A couple of times she thought she actually saw it, but perhaps that was only the sun moving through the tree-branches. She did not want to see it; she had seen all that she wanted to in that single flash of lightning the night before. The fur of it, the enormous cocked ears of it, the hulk of it.

The eyes, too. Those black eyes, big and inhuman. Glassy but aware. Aware of *her*.

It won't leave until it's sure I can't get out, she thought wearily. *It's not going to let that happen. It's not going to let me get away.*

Shortly after noon she saw that the puddles in the road-ruts were drying up and replenished her water supply while she could, straining the water through her hat and into the hood of her poncho, then pouring it into the plastic bottles. The water still had a hazy, dirty look, but such things no longer caused her much concern. She thought if woods-water was going to kill her, she probably would have died when it first made her sick. What *did* concern her was lack of food. She ate all but the last few nuts and berries after filling her bottles; by breakfast tomorrow she would be scrounging at the bottom of the pack, as she had scrounged for the last few potato chips. She might find more stuff alongside the road, but she wasn't hopeful.

The road went on and on, sometimes fading a little and sometimes clarifying for a few hundred yards. For awhile bushes grew up on the crown between the ruts. Trisha thought they were blackberry bushes – they looked like the ones from which she and her Mom had picked hatfuls of fresh sweet berries in the Sanford toy woods, but it was a month too early for blackberries. She also saw mushrooms, but did not trust any enough to eat them. They weren't in her mother's field of knowledge, nor had they studied them in school. In school they had learned about nuts and not taking rides from strangers (because some strangers were nuts), but not mushrooms. The one thing she was sure of was that you would die – and horribly – if you ate the wrong kind. And skipping them was really no big sacrifice. She now had little appetite, and her throat was sore.

Around four in the afternoon she stumbled over a log, fell on her side, tried to get up, and found she couldn't. Her legs were trembling and felt as weak as water. She took off her pack (struggling with it for an alarming length of time), and finally got free of it. She ate all but the last two or three beechnuts, almost gagging up the last one she attempted. She fought for it and won, stretching her neck like a baby bird and double-gulping. She tamped it down (at least for the time being) with a swig of warm, gritty water.

'Red Sox time,' she muttered, and dug out her Walkman. She doubted if she could pick them up, but it wouldn't hurt to try; it would be one o'clock or so on the West Coast, a sure day game, and just starting.

There was nothing at all on the FM band, not even a faint whisper of music. On the AM she found a man babbling rapidly away in French (he chuckled as he did so, which was disquieting), and then, down near 1600, at the very foot of the dial, a miracle: faint but audible, the voice of Joe Castiglione.

'All right, Valentin leads away from second,' he said. 'The three-one pitch . . . *and Garciaparra hits a long high drive to deep center field! It's back . . . it's GONE! Red Sox lead, two to nothing!*'

'Way to go, Nomar, you the man,' Trisha said in a hoarse, croaky voice she hardly recognized as her own, and pumped her fist weakly at the sky. O'Leary struck out and the inning ended. '*Who do you call when your WINDshield's BUSted?*' sang voices from a world far away, one where there were paths everywhere and all gods worked behind the scenes.

'1-800,' Trisha began. '54 . . .'

She trailed off before she could finish. As her doze deepened she slid further and further to her right, coughing from time to time. The coughs had a deep, phlegmy sound. During the fifth inning, something came to the edge of the woods and looked at her. Flies and noseeums made a cloud around its rudiment of a face. In the specious brilliance of its eyes was a complete history of nothing. It stood there for a long time. At last it pointed at her with one razor-claw hand – *she is mine, she is my property* – and backed into the woods again.

BOTTOM OF THE NINTH

At some point late in the game, Trisha thought she came briefly, blearily awake. Jerry Trupiano was announcing – it *sounded* like Troop, at least, but he was saying that the Seattle Monsters had the bases loaded and Gordon was trying to close the game out. 'That thing at the plate's a killer,' Troop said, 'and Gordon looks afraid for the first time this year. Where's God when you need him, Joe?'

'Danvizz,' Joe Castiglione said. 'Crying real tizz.'
Surely that was a dream, had to have been – one that might or might not have been mixed with a little smidge of reality. All Trisha knew for sure was that when she next awoke completely, the sun was almost down, she was feverish, her throat hurt badly each time she swallowed, and her radio was ominously quiet.

'Fell asleep with it on, you stupid thing,' she said in her new croaky voice. 'You big dumb asshole.' She looked at the top of the case, hoping to see the little red light, hoping she had just moved the tuning by accident when she started sliding off to one side (she had awakened with her head cocked against one shoulder and her neck aching fiercely), knowing better. And sure enough, the red light was out.

She tried to tell herself the batteries couldn't have lasted much longer, anyway, but it didn't help and she cried some more. Knowing the radio was dead made her feel sad, so sad. It was like losing your last friend. Moving slowly and creakily, she stowed the radio back in her pack, did the buckles, and put the pack back on. It was almost empty, yet seemed to weigh a ton. How could that be?

I'm on a road, at least, she reminded herself. *I'm on a road.* But now, with the light of another day slipping out of the sky, not even that seemed to help. *Road, shmoad,* she thought. The fact of it actually seemed to mock her, began to seem like a blown save opportunity, somehow – like when a team got just an out or two away from sewing up the win and then the roof fell in. The stupid road could go on through these woods for another hundred and forty miles, for all she knew, and at the end of it there might be nothing; just another scruff of bushes or another hideous bog.

Nevertheless she began to walk again, slowly and wearily, with her head down and her shoulders so slumped that the pack-straps kept trying to slip off like the straps of a shell did if the top was too big. Only with a shell top, you only had to brush the straps back up. With the pack-straps you first had to *pick* and then *lift*.

About a half hour before full dark, one of them slipped off her shoulder entirely and the pack came askew. Trisha thought briefly of just letting the damned thing fall and walking on without it. She might have done just that if there had only been the last handful of checkerberries inside. But there was the water, and the water, gritty as it was, soothed her throat. She decided to stop for the night instead.

She knelt down on the crown of the road, slipped off the pack with a sigh of relief, then lay down with her head on it. She looked at the dark mass of the woods to her right.

'You just stay away,' she said as clearly as she could. 'Stay away or I'll dial 1-800 and call the giant. Do you understand me?'

Something heard her. It might or might not understand, and it did not reply, but it was there. She could feel it. Was it still letting her ripen? Feeding on her fear before it came out to feed on her? If so, the game was almost over. She was nearly out of fear. She thought suddenly of calling to it again, of telling it she didn't mean what she'd just said, that she was tired and it could come get her if it wanted. But she didn't do it. She was afraid that it might take her up on it if she did.

She drank a little water and looked up at the sky. She thought of Bork the Dork saying the God of Tom Gordon couldn't be bothered with her, that He had other fish to fry. Trisha doubted if that was exactly so . . . but He wasn't here, that seemed certain. Maybe it wasn't *couldn't* so much as *wouldn't*. Bork the Dork had also said, *I must admit he is a sports fan . . . not necessarily a Red Sox fan, however.*

Trisha took off her Red Sox cap — now battered and sweatstained and smeared with bits of the forest — and ran her finger across the bent brim. Her best thing. Her father had gotten Tom Gordon to sign it for her, had sent it to Fenway Park with a letter saying Tom was his daughter's favorite player, and Tom (or his accredited representative) had sent it back in the stamped, self-addressed envelope her father had provided, autographed across the visor. She guessed it was still her best thing. Other than some murky water, a handful of dried, tasteless berries, and her dirty clothes, it was just about her *only* thing. And now the signature was gone, blurred to nothing but a black shadow by rain and her own sweaty hands. But it had been there, and she was *still* here – for the time being, at least.

'God, if You can't be a Red Sox fan, be a Tom Gordon fan,' she said. 'Can you do that much, at least? Can you *be* that much?'

She dozed in and out of consciousness all night, shivering, falling asleep and then snapping awake, sure that it was there with her, *It,* that it had finally come out of the woods to take her. Tom Gordon spoke to her; once her father also spoke to her. He stood right behind her, asking her if she'd like some macaroons, but when she turned around no one was there. More meteors burned across the sky, but she couldn't tell for sure if they were really there or if she was only dreaming them. Once she took out her radio, hoping the batteries had come back a little – sometimes they did, if you gave them a chance to rest – but she dropped it into the high grass before she could check and then couldn't find it no matter how much she combed her fingers through the tangles. Eventually her hands returned to her pack and felt the straps still threaded snugly through the buckles. Trisha decided she had never taken the radio out in the first place, because she never could have refixed the buckles and straps so neatly in the dark. She hacked her way through a dozen coughing fits, and now they hurt way down in her ribcage. At some point she hoisted herself up enough to pee, and what came out was hot enough to burn and make her bite her lips.

The night passed as nights of deepening sickness always do; time grew soft and strange. When the birds at last began to chirrup and she saw a little light beginning to strain through the trees, Trisha could hardly believe it. She lifted her hands and looked at her dirty fingers. She could hardly believe she was still alive, either, but it seemed she was.

She stayed put until the day was light enough to see the ever-present cloud of bugs around her head. Then she got slowly up and waited to see if her legs were going to support her or give way and spill her back down again.

If they do I'll crawl, she thought, but she didn't have to crawl, not yet; they held her. She bent and hooked a hand into one of the pack-straps. When she straightened back up again, dizziness roared through her and a squadron of those black-winged butterflies clouded her sight. At last they faded and she managed to get the pack on.

Then there was another problem – which way had she been going? She was no longer entirely sure, and the road looked the same in both directions. She stepped away from the log, looking uncertainly back and forth. Her foot clipped something. It was her Walkman, all tangled up in the earphone cord and wet with dew. Apparently she had taken it out after all. She bent down, picked it up, and looked at it stupidly. Was she going to take off the pack again, open it, and put the Walkman back inside? That seemed too hard – on a par with moving a mountain. On the other hand, throwing it away seemed wrong, like admitting she had given up.

Trisha stood where she was for three minutes or more, looking down at the little radio-tape player with her fever-bright eyes. Throw it away or keep it? Throw it away or keep it? What's your decision, Patricia, do you want to stick with the waterless cookware or go for the car, the mink coat, and the trip to Rio? It occurred to her that if she were her brother Pete's Mac PowerBook, she'd be throwing up error messages and little bomb icons all over the place. She was startled into a laugh at this image.

The laughter almost immediately turned into coughing. It was the worst bout by far, doubling her over. Soon she was barking like a dog with her hands planted just above her knees and her hanging hair swaying back and forth in a filthy curtain. She somehow kept her feet, refusing to give in and fall, and as the coughing fit was tapering off, she realized that she ought to clip the Walkman to the waistband of her jeans. That was what the clip on the back of the case was for, wasn't it? Sure, you bet. What an El Dopo she was.

She opened her mouth to say, *Elementary, my dear Watson* – she and Pepsi sometimes said that to each other – and when she did, something wet and warm came slobbering out over her lower lip. She wiped up a palmful of bright red blood and looked at it, her eyes widening.

I must have bit something in my mouth when I was coughing, she thought, and immediately knew better. This had come from deeper inside. The idea scared her, and fright brought the world into sharper focus. She found herself able to think again. She cleared her throat (gently; it hurt too much to do it any other way) and then spat. Bright red. Oh jeez, Louise, but there was nothing she could do about it now, and at least she was clearheaded enough to figure out how to make sure of her direction on the road. The sun had gone down on her right. She turned now until the rising sun was winking through the trees on her left, and immediately saw she was pointed the right way. She didn't know how she could have been confused in the first place.

Slowly, gingerly, like someone walking on a freshly rinsed tile floor, Trisha got moving again. *This is probably it,* she thought. *Today's probably my last chance, maybe even this morning's my last chance. I may be too weak and sick to walk by this afternoon, and if I can get on my feet after another night out here, it'll be a blue-eyed miracle.*

Blue-eyed miracle. Was that her mother's or her father's?

'Who gives a rat's ass?' Trisha croaked. 'If I get out of this, I'm going to make up some sayings of my own.'

Fifty or sixty feet north of the place where she had spent that endless Sunday night and Monday morning, Trisha realized she still had her Walkman in her right hand. She stopped and went carefully and laboriously about the task of getting it clipped to her waistband. Her jeans were absolutely floating on her now, and she could see the sharp jut of her hipbones. *Lose a few more pounds and I'll be able to model the latest Paris fashions,* she thought. She was just wondering what to do with the headphone attachment when a sudden rough rattle of distant explosions split the still morning air — it sounded like a puddle of soda being sucked up through a giant straw.

Trisha cried out, and she was not alone in her startlement; a number of crows cawed, and a pheasant exploded through the brush in a ruffled whir of indignation.

Trisha stood, wide-eyed, the forgotten earbud headphones penduluming at the end of their cord by her scabby, dirty left ankle. She knew that sound; it was the rattle of backfires through an old muffler. A truck, maybe, or some kid's bucket of rods. There was another road up there. A *real* road.

She wanted to run and knew she must not. If she did, she would blow out all her energy in one burst. That would be dreadful. To faint away and perhaps die of exposure within actual sound of traffic would be like blowing the save when the opposing team was down to their last strike. Such abominations happened, but she would not let it happen to her.

She began to walk instead, forcing herself to move slowly and deliberately, listening all the while for another series of those rattling backfires, or a distant engine, or a horn. There was nothing, nothing at all, and after an hour of walking she began to think she had hallucinated the whole thing. This hadn't seemed like a hallucination, but . . .

She topped a rise and looked down. She began coughing again, and more blood flew from her lips, bright in the sun, but Trisha took no notice – did not even put her hand up. Below her the rutted track she was on ended, T-squaring into a dirt road.

Trisha walked slowly down and stood upon it. She could see no tire tracks – it was hardpan – but there were real ruts here, and no grass growing down the middle. The new road ran at right angles to her road, roughly east and west. And here, at last, Trisha made the right decision. She did not turn west for any other reason than that her head had begun to ache again and she didn't want to be walking directly into the sunshine . . . but she *did* turn west. Four miles from where she stood, New Hampshire Route 96, a patched ribbon of hot-top, ran through the woods. A few cars and a great many pulp-trucks used this road; it was one of the latter which Trisha had heard backing off through its ancient exhaust system as the driver downshifted for Kemongus Hill. The sound had carried better than nine miles through the still morning air.

She began to move again, and with a new feeling of strength. It was perhaps forty-five minutes later that she heard something, distant but unmistakable.

Don't be stupid, you've gotten to a place where anything's *mistakable.*

Perhaps so, but . . .

She cocked her head like the dog on Gramma McFarland's old records, the ones Gramma kept up in the attic. She held her breath. She heard the thump of blood in her temples, the wheeze of her breath in her infected throat, the call of birds, the rustle of the breeze. She heard the hum of mosquitoes around her ears . . . and another hum, as well. The hum of tires on pavement. Very distant, but there.

Trisha began to cry. 'Please don't let me be making it up,' she said in a husky voice that was now down to little more than a whisper. 'Aw, God, please, don't let me be making that u—'

A louder rustling noise commenced behind her – not the breeze, not this time. Even if she might have convinced herself (for a few cruddy seconds or so) that it was, what about the snapping sound of branches? And then the grinding, splintering sound of something falling – a small tree, probably, that had been in the way. In *Its* way. It had let her get this close to rescue, had allowed her to come within actual hearing of the path she had so casually and carelessly lost. It had watched her painful progress, perhaps with amusement, perhaps with some sort of god's compassion that was too terrible to even think about. Now it was through watching, through waiting.

Slowly, both with terror and with a strange sort of calm inevitability, Trisha turned to face the God of the Lost.

BOTTOM OF THE NINTH:
SAVE SITUATION

It emerged from the trees on the left side of the road, and Trisha's first thought was: *Is that all? Is that all it ever was?* Grown men would have turned and run from the *Ursus americanus* which lumbered out of the last screen of bushes – it was a fully grown North American black bear, perhaps four hundred pounds – but Trisha had been prepared for some awful horror torn from the underside of the night.

There were leaves and burdocks caught in its shiny fur, and held in one hand – yes, it had a hand, the clawed rudiment of one, at least – was a branch from which most of the bark had been stripped. It held this like a woodsy wand or scepter. It came to the middle of the road, seeming almost to paddle from side to side. It remained on all fours for a moment, and then, with a soft grunt, rose to a stand on its rear legs. When it did, Trisha saw it was not a black bear at all. She had been right the first time. It looked a little like a bear, but it was really the God of the Lost, and it had come for her.

It peered at her with black eyes that were not eyes at all but only sockets. Its tan muzzle scented at the air, and then it raised the broken branch it held to its mouth. The muzzle wrinkled back, revealing a double row of huge, green-stained teeth. It sucked at the end of its branch, reminding her of a little kid with a lollipop. Then, with great deliberation, the teeth clenched upon it and tore it in two. The woods had fallen silent, and she heard the sound its teeth made very clearly, a sound like splintering bone. It was the sound her arm would make, if that thing bit down on it. *When* it bit down on it.

It stretched its neck, its ears flicking, and Trisha saw it moved in its own small dark galaxy of minges and noseeums, just as she did. Its shadow, long in the morning light, stretched almost to Trisha's scuffed sneakers. They were no more than sixty feet apart.

It had come for her.

Run, called the God of the Lost. *Run from me, race me to the road. This bear's body is slow, not yet filled with a summer's forage; pickings have been slim. Run. Perhaps I'll let you live.*

Yes, run! she thought, and then, immediately came the cold voice of the tough tootsie: *You can't run. You can barely stand up, sweetheart.*

The thing that wasn't a bear stood looking at her, ears flicking at the bugs which surrounded its big triangular head, sides shining with healthy fur. It held the stump of its stick in one clawed paw. Its jaws moved with ruminative slowness, and little shredded splinters dribbled out between its teeth. Some fell, some stuck to its muzzle. Its eyes were sockets lined with minuscule buzzing life – maggots and wriggling baby flies, mosquito larvae and God knew what else, a living soup that made her think of the swamp she had walked through.

I killed the deer. I watched you, and drew my circle around you. Run from me. Worship me with your feet and I may let you live.

208

The woods lay silent all about them, breathing their sour urgent scent of green. Her breath rasped softly in and out of her sick throat. The thing that looked like a bear gazed down on her haughtily from its seven feet of height. Its head was in the sky and its claws held the earth. Trisha looked back at it, up at it, and understood what she must do.

She must close.

It's God's nature to come on in the bottom of the ninth, Tom had told her. And what was the secret to closing? Establishing who was better. You could be beaten . . . but you must not beat yourself.

First, though, you had to create that stillness. The one that came from the shoulders and spun about the body until it was a cocoon of certainty. You could be beaten, but you must not beat yourself. You couldn't serve up a fat pitch and you couldn't run.

'Icewater,' she said, and the thing standing in the middle of the dirt road tilted its head so it looked like an enormous listening dog. It cocked its ears forward. Trisha reached up, turned her cap the right way around, and pulled the curved visor low on her brow. Wearing it the way Tom Gordon did. Then she pivoted her body so it was facing the right side of the road and took a step forward so her legs were apart, left leg pointed at the bear-thing. Her face remained turned toward it as she stepped; she fixed her gaze on the eyesockets looking through the dancing cloud of bugs. *It all comes down to this,* Joe Castiglione said; *everybody fasten your seatbelts.*

'Come on, if you're coming,' Trisha called to it. She pulled the Walkman off the waistband of her jeans, yanked the cord free, and dropped the earbuds at her feet. The Walkman went behind her back and she began to turn it in her fingers, looking for the right grip. 'I've got icewater in my veins and I hope yoú freeze on the first bite. Come on, you busher! Batter-fucking-up!'

The bear-thing let go of its stick and then dropped back onto all fours. It pawed at the hardpan surface of the road like a restless bull, digging up clods of earth with its claws, and then moved toward her, waddling with surprising, deceptive speed. As it came, it laid its ears flat against its skull. Its muzzle wrinkled back, and from within its mouth Trisha heard a droning sound which she recognized at once: not bees but wasps. It had taken the shape of a bear on its outside, but on the inside it was truer; inside it was full of wasps. Of course it was. Hadn't the blackrobe by the stream been its prophet?

Run, it said as it came toward her, its big hindquarters swaying from side to side. It was weirdly graceful, leaving clawed prints behind and a scatter of droppings on the surface of the packed earth. *Run, it's your last chance.*

Except it was stillness that was her last chance.

Stillness and maybe a good hard curveball.

Trisha put her hands together, coming to the set. The Walkman no longer felt like a Walkman; it felt like a baseball. There were no Fenway Faithful here, rising to their feet in the Boston Church of Baseball; no rhythmic clapping; no umpires and no batboy. There was only her and the green stillness and the hot morning sunshine and a thing that looked like a bear on the outside and was full of wasps on the inside. Only stillness and now she understood how someone like Tom Gordon must feel, standing in the set position in the silence of the cyclone's core, where all pressure falls to zero and all sounds are shut out and it all comes down to this: fasten your seatbelts.

She stood in the set position and let the stillness spin out around her. Yes, it came from the shoulders. Let it eat her; let it beat her. It could do both. But she would not beat herself.

And I won't run.

It stopped before her and stretched its neck up so its face approached her face as if to kiss. There were no eyes, only two squirming circles, wormhole universes filled with breeding bugs. They hummed and squirmed and jostled each other for position in the tunnels that bored toward the god's unimaginable brain. Its mouth opened and she saw that its throat was lined with wasps, plump ungainly poison factories crawling over the remains of a chewed stick and the pinkish lump of deergut that served as its tongue. Its breath was the muddy stink of the bog.

She saw these things, noted them briefly, then looked beyond. Veritek flashed the sign. Soon she would make her pitch, but for now she was still. She was still. Let the batter wait, anticipate, lose his timing; let him wonder, begin to think his guess about the curve was wrong.

The bear-creature sniffed delicately all around her face. Bugs crawled in and out of its nostrils. Noseeums fluttered between the two locked faces, one furry and the other smooth. Minges flicked against the damp surfaces of Trisha's open, unblinking eyes. The thing's rudiment of a face was shifting and changing, always shifting and changing – it was the face of teachers and friends; it was the face of parents and brothers; it was the face of the man who might come and offer you a ride when you were walking home from school. Stranger-danger was what they had been taught in the first grade: stranger-danger. It stank of death and disease and everything random; the hum of its poisoned works was, she thought, the *real* Subaudible.

It rose up on its back legs again, swaying a little as if to beast-music only it could hear, and then it swatted at her . . . yet it was playful, only playful as yet, missing her face by several inches. The passage of its earth-darkened claws breezed the hair off her forehead. The hair settled back light as milkweed puffs but Trisha did not move. She stood in the set position, looking through the bear's underbelly, where a bluish-white blaze of fur grew in a shape like a lightning bolt.

Look at me.

No.

Look at me!

It was as if unseen hands had grasped her beneath the angles of her jaw. Slowly, not wanting to but helpless to resist, Trisha raised her head. She looked up. She looked into the bear-thing's empty eyes and understood it meant to kill her no matter what. Courage was not enough. But so what? If a little courage was all you had, so what? It was time to close.

Without thinking about it, Trisha brought her left foot back against her right one and went into her motion – not the one her Dad had taught her in the back yard but the one she'd learned on TV, watching Gordon. When she stepped forward again and raised her right hand to her right ear and then beyond – really rearing back because this would be no lazy offspeed pitch, no eephus; this was going to be the heartbreaker, the serious bent cheese – the bear-thing took a clumsy, overbalanced step backward. Did the squirming things which lent it its dim vision register the baseball in her hand as a weapon? Or was it the threatening, aggressive motion which startled it – the raised hand, the stepping forward when she should have been stepping back and turning to run? It didn't matter. The thing grunted in what might have been perplexity. A little cloud of wasps puffed out of its mouth like living vapor. It waved one furry foreleg in an effort to keep its balance. As it struggled to stay on its feet, a shot rang out.

The man in the woods that morning, the first human being to see Trisha McFarland in nine days, was too shaken to even try lying to the police about why he had been in the woods with a high-powered autoload rifle; he'd been in the market for an out-of-season deer. His name was Travis Herrick, and he didn't believe in spending money on food if he didn't have to. There were too many other important things to spend money on – lottery tickets and beer, for instance. In any case, he was never tried for anything, or even fined, and he did not kill the creature he saw standing in front of the little girl, who faced it so still and so brave-like.

'If she'da moved when it first come up to her, it woulda tore her apart,' Herrick said. 'It's a wonder it didn't tear her apart anyways. She musta stared it down, just like Tarzan in them old jungle movies. I come over the rise and see the two of em, I musta stood there watchin em for twenty seconds at least. Might even have been a minute, you lose all track of time in a situation like that, but I couldn't shoot. They 'us too close together. I was afraid of hittin the girl. Then she moved. She had somethin in her hand and she went to throw it at im almost like she was pitchin a baseball. Her movin like that startled it. It stepped back and kinda lost its balance. I knew right there was the only chance that little girl had, so I lifted up my gun and I shot.'

No trial, no fine. What Travis Herrick got was his own float in Grafton Notch's 1998 Fourth of July parade. Yeah, baby.

Trisha heard the gunshot, knew it at once for what it was, and saw one of the thing's cocked ears suddenly fly apart at the very tip like a piece of shredded paper. She could see momentary squiglets of blue sky through the torn flaps; she also saw a scatter of red droplets, no bigger than checkerberries, fly into the air in an arc. At the same instant she saw that the bear was just a bear again, its eyes big and glassy and almost comically surprised. Or perhaps it had been a bear all along.

Except she knew better than that.

She continued with her motion, flinging the baseball. It struck the bear dead-bang between the eyes and – whoa, hey, talk about hallucinations – she saw a couple of Energizer double A batteries fall out of it onto the road.

'*Strike three called!*' she screamed, and at the sound of her hoarse, triumphant, breaking voice, the wounded bear turned and fled, lumbering on all fours, quickly picking up speed, shedding blood from its torn ear as it got into an all-out fanny-wagging run. There was another whipcrack gunshot, and Trisha felt the slug buffet the air as it passed less than a foot to her right. It dug up a puff of road dust well behind the bear, which veered to its left and plunged back into the woods. For a moment she could see the gleam of its shiny black pelt, then small trees shaking as if in a parody of fear as it passed among them, and then the bear was gone.

She turned, staggering, and saw a small man in patched green pants, green gumrubber boots, and an old flapping T-shirt running toward her. His head was bald on top; long hair flapped down on either side and hung on his shoulders; little rimless eyeglasses flashed in the sun. He was carrying a rifle high over his head, like a raiding Indian in an old movie. She wasn't a bit surprised to see that his shirt had the Red Sox emblem on it. Every man in New England had at least one Sox shirt, it seemed.

'*Hey girlie!*' he screamed. '*Hey girlie, Jesus, are you all right? Christ almighty, that was a fucking BEAR, are you all right?*'

Trisha staggered toward him. 'Strike three called,' she said, but the words hardly reached beyond her own mouth. She had used up most of what she had with that last scream. All that remained was a kind of bleeding whisper. 'Strike three called, I threw the curve and just froze him.'

'What?' He stopped in front of her. 'I can't make you out, honey, come again.'

'Did you see?' she asked, meaning the pitch she had thrown – that unbelievable curve that hadn't just broken but snapped like a whip. 'Did you *see* it?'

'I . . . I saw . . .' But in truth he didn't know *what* he had seen. There had been a few seconds in that frozen time when the girl and the bear had been regarding each other that he hadn't been sure, not entirely sure it *was* a bear, but that he never told anyone. Folks knew he drank; they would think he was crazy. And all he saw now was a delirious little girl who looked like nothing but a stick-figure held together by dirt and ragged clothes. He couldn't remember her name but he knew who she was; it had been on the radio and the TV, as well. He had no idea how she could possibly have gotten so far north and west, but he knew perfectly well who she was.

Trisha stumbled over her own feet and would have fallen to the road if Herrick hadn't caught her. When he did, his rifle − a .350 Krag that was the pride of his life − discharged again, close to her ear, deafening her. Trisha hardly noticed. It all seemed normal, somehow.

'Did you see?' she asked again, not able to hear her own voice, not even completely sure if she was actually speaking. The little man looked bewildered and scared and not especially bright, but she thought he also looked kind. 'I got him with the curve, froze him, did you see?'

His lips were moving, but she couldn't tell what he was saying. He put the rifle down on the road, though, and that was a relief. He picked her up and turned her so fast it made her dizzy − she probably would have thrown up if there had been anything left in her stomach. She began to cough. She couldn't hear that, either, not with that monstrous ringing in her ears, but she could feel it, way down in her chest and ribcage, *pulling*.

She wanted to tell him she was glad to be carried, glad to be rescued, but she also wanted to tell him that the bear-thing had been backing away even before he fired his gun. She had seen the bewilderment in its face, had seen its fear of her when she went from the set to the motion. She wanted to tell this man who was now running with her one thing, one very *important* thing, but he was jouncing

216

her and she was coughing and her head was ringing and she couldn't tell if she was saying it or not.

Trisha was still trying to say *I got it, I got the save* when she passed out.

POSTGAME

She was in the woods again and she came to a clearing she knew. Standing in the middle of it, by the stump that wasn't a stump but a gatepost with a rusty ringbolt embedded in the top, was Tom Gordon. He was idly flicking the ringbolt back and forth.

I already had this dream, she thought, but as she approached him, she saw it had changed in one particular: instead of the gray road uniform, Tom was wearing his white home uniform, with Number 36 on the back in bright red silk. So the road trip was over. The Sox were at Fenway again, back at home, and the road trip was over. Except she and Tom were here; they were back in this clearing.

'Tom?' she said timidly.

He looked at her, eyebrows raised. Back and forth went the rusty ringbolt between his talented fingers. Back and forth.

'I closed.'

'I know you did, honey,' he said. 'You did a good job.'

Back and forth, back and forth. Who do you call when your ringbolt's busted?

'How much of it was real?'

'All of it,' he said, as if it didn't really matter. And then, again: 'You did a good job.'

'I was stupid to get off the path like I did, wasn't I?'

219

He looked at her with slight surprise, then pushed up his cap with the hand that wasn't flipping the ringbolt back and forth. He smiled, and when he smiled he looked young. 'What path?' he said.

'Trisha?' That was a woman's voice, coming from behind her. It sounded like her mother's voice, but what would Mom be doing out here in the woods?

'She probably doesn't hear you,' said another woman. This voice she didn't know.

Trisha turned. The woods were darkening, the shapes of the trees blurring together, becoming unreal, like a backdrop. Shapes moved there and she felt a momentary prick of fear. *The wasp-priest,* she thought. *It's the wasp-priest, he's coming back.*

Then she realized she was dreaming and the fear passed. She turned back to Tom, but he was no longer there, only the splintered post with the ringbolt in the top . . . and his warmup jacket lying in the grass. GORDON printed across the back.

She glimpsed him on the far side of the clearing, a white shape like a ghost. 'Trisha, what's God's nature?' he called.

To come on in the bottom of the ninth, she wanted to say, but no sound came out.

'Look,' her mother said. 'Her lips are moving!'

'Trish?' That was Pete, sounding anxious and hopeful. 'Trish, are you awake?'

She opened her eyes and the woods rolled away into some darkness which would never entirely leave her now – *What path?* She was in a hospital room. There was a thing up her nose and something else – a tube – running into her hand. Her chest felt very heavy, very full. Standing by her bed was her father, her mother, her brother. Behind them, looming large and white, was the nurse who had said *she probably doesn't hear you.*

'Trisha,' her Mom said. She was crying. Trisha saw that Pete was also crying. 'Trisha, honey. Oh honey.' She took Trisha's hand, the one without the thing in it.

Trisha tried to smile, but her mouth was too heavy to go up, even at the corners. She moved her eyes and saw her Red Sox hat on the seat of the chair by her bed. Smeared across the visor was a dim blackish-gray shadow. Once it had been Tom Gordon's signature.

Dad, she tried to say. Nothing came out but a cough. It was only a little cough, but it hurt enough to make her wince.

'Don't try to talk, Patricia,' the nurse said, and Trisha could tell both by the nurse's tone and posture that she wanted the family out of here; in another moment she would make them leave. 'You're a sick girl. You've got pneumonia. Both lungs.'

Her Mom seemed to hear none of this. She was sitting on the bed beside her now, stroking Trisha's wasted arm. She wasn't sobbing, but tears welled steadily from her eyes and rolled down her cheeks. Pete stood next to her, crying in the same silent fashion. Trisha was touched by his tears in a way she wasn't by her mother's, but she still thought Pete looked quite remarkably dorky. Beside him, beside the chair, stood her Dad.

This time Trisha didn't try to speak, only fixed her father with her eyes and mouthed it again, very carefully: *Dad!*

He saw and bent forward. 'What, honey? What is it?'

'I think that's enough,' the nurse said. 'All her signs are up, and we don't want that – she's had all the excitement she needs for awhile. If you'll just help me out, now . . . help *her* out—'

Mom got to her feet. 'We love you, Trish. Thank God you're safe. We'll be here, but you need to sleep now. Larry, let's—'

He took no notice of Quilla. He remained bent over Trisha, fingers lightly tented on the sheet. 'What is it, Trish? What do you want?'

She moved her eyes to the chair, to his face, back to the chair. He looked puzzled – she was sure he wasn't going to get it – and then his face cleared. He smiled, turned, picked up the hat, and tried to put it on her head.

She raised the hand her mother had caressed – it weighed a ton, but she managed. Then she opened the fingers. Closed them. Opened them.

'Okay, hon. Okay, right.'

He put the cap in her hand, and when she closed her fingers on the visor, he kissed them. Trisha began to cry at that, as soundlessly as her mother and brother.

'All right,' the nurse said. 'That's it. You'll really have to—'

Trisha looked at the nurse and shook her head.

'What?' the nurse asked. 'What *now*? Goodness' sake!'

Trisha slowly transferred the cap to the hand with the IV needle in it. She looked at her father as she did it, making sure he was looking at her. She was tired. Soon she would sleep. But not yet. Not until she had said what she had to say.

He was watching, watching closely. Good.

She reached across her body with her right hand, never taking her eyes from her father, because he was the one who would know; if he understood, he would translate.

Trisha tapped the visor of her cap, then pointed her right index finger up at the ceiling.

The smile which lit his face from the eyes down was the sweetest, truest thing she had ever seen. If there was a path, it was there. Trisha closed her own eyes on his understanding and floated away into sleep.

Game over.

AUTHOR'S POSTSCRIPT

First, I took some liberties with the Red Sox's 1998 schedule . . . small ones, I assure you.

There is a real Tom Gordon, who does indeed pitch in the closer's role for the Boston Red Sox, but the Gordon in this story is fictional. The impressions fans have of people who have achieved some degree of celebrity are *always* fictional, as I can attest of my own personal experience. In one particular the real Gordon and Trisha's version of him are the same: both point skyward after the final out of a successful save has been recorded.

In 1998 Tom 'Flash' Gordon recorded forty-four saves to lead the American League. Forty-three of them came consecutively, an American League record. Gordon's season came to an unfortunate conclusion, however; as Bork the Dork says, God may be a sports fan, but He doesn't seem to be a Red Sox fan. In Game Four of the Divisional Playoff against the Indians, Gordon surrendered three hits and two runs. The Red Sox lost, 2–1. It was Gordon's first blown save in five months, and it ended the Red Sox's 1998 season. It did not, however, detract from Gordon's extraordinary accomplishments – without those forty-four saves, the Red Sox probably would have finished fourth in their division instead of winning ninety-one games and compiling the American League's second-best record in 1998. There's a saying, one that most closers like Tom Gordon would probably agree with: some days you eat the bear . . . and some days the bear eats you.

The things Trisha eats to stay alive can indeed be found in the woods of northern New England during the late spring season; had she not been a town girl, she might have found lots more supplies — more nuts, roots, even cattails. My friend Joe Floyd helped me with this part of it, and it was Joe who told me that fiddleheads grow right into early July in the marshes of the northern backwoods.

The woods themselves are real. If you should visit them on your vacation, bring a compass, bring good maps . . . and try to stay on the path.

STEPHEN KING
Longboat Key, Florida
February 1, 1999

STEPHEN KING

FULL DARK, NO STARS

Is it possible to fully know anyone? Even those we love the most? What tips someone over the edge to commit a crime?

For a Nebraska farmer, the turning point comes when his wife threatens to sell off the family homestead.

A cozy mystery writer plots a savage revenge after a brutal encounter with a stranger.

Harry Streeter gets the chance to cure himself from illness – if he agrees to impose misery on an old rival.

And Darcy Anderson discovers a box containing her husband's dark and terrifying secrets – he's not just the man who keeps his nails short and collects coins. And now he's heading home . . .

'Fine stories to take with us into the night' – Neil Gaiman, *Guardian*

'An extraordinary collection, thrillingly merciless and a career high point' – Matt Thorne, *Sunday Telegraph*

Turn the page to read an extract . . .

Copyright © 2010 by Stephen King. 'Under the Weather' copyright ©
2011 by Stephen King

First published in Great Britain in 2010 by Hodder & Stoughton
An Hachette UK Company

This paperback edition published 2011

The right of Stephen King to be identified as the Author
of the Work has been asserted by him in accordance with the
Copyright, Designs and Patents Act 1988.

1

A CIP catalogue record for this title is
available from the British Library

A format paperback ISBN 978 1 444 71257 5
B format paperback ISBN 978 1 444 71256 8

Typeset in Bembo by
Palimpsest Book Production Limited, Falkirk, Stirlingshire

Printed and bound by Clays Ltd, Elcograf S.p.A.

Hodder & Stoughton policy is to use papers that are natural,
renewable and recyclable products and made from wood grown
in sustainable forests. The logging and manufacturing processes
are expected to conform to the environmental regulations
of the country of origin

Hodder & Stoughton
Carmelite House
50 Victoria Embankment
London EC4Y 0DZ

www.hodder.co.uk

1

The one thing nobody asked in casual conversation, Darcy thought in the days after she found what she found in the garage, was this: *How's your marriage?* They asked *how was your weekend* and *how was your trip to Florida* and *how's your health* and *how are the kids*; they even asked *how's life been treatin you, hon?* But nobody asked *how's your marriage?*

Good, she would have answered the question before that night. *Everything's fine.*

She had been born Darcellen Madsen (Darcellen, a name only parents besotted with a freshly purchased book of baby names could love), in the year John F. Kennedy was elected President. She was raised in Freeport, Maine, back when it was a town instead of an adjunct to L.L.Bean, America's first superstore, and half a dozen other oversized retail operations of the sort that are called 'outlets' (as if they were sewer drains rather than shopping locations). She went to Freeport High School, and then to Addison Business School, where she learned secretarial skills. She was hired by Joe Ransome Chevrolet, which by 1984, when she left the company, was the largest car dealership in Portland. She was plain, but with the help of two marginally more sophisticated girlfriends, learned enough makeup skills to make herself pretty on workdays and downright eye-catching on Friday and Saturday nights, when a bunch of them liked to go out for margaritas at The Lighthouse or Mexican Mike's (where there was live music).

In 1982, Joe Ransome hired a Portland accounting firm

to help him figure out his tax situation, which had become complicated ('The kind of problem you want to have,' Darcy overheard him tell one of the senior salesmen). A pair of briefcase-toting men came out, one old and one young. Both wore glasses and conservative suits; both combed their short hair neatly away from their foreheads in a way that made Darcy think of the photographs in her mother's MEMORIES OF '54 senior yearbook, the one with the image of a boy cheerleader holding a megaphone to his mouth stamped on its faux-leather cover.

The younger accountant was Bob Anderson. She got talking with him on their second day at the dealership, and in the course of their conversation, asked him if he had any hobbies. Yes, he said, he was a numismatist.

He started to tell her what that was and she said, 'I know. My father collects Lady Liberty dimes and buffalo-head nickels. He says they're his numismatical hobby-horse. Do you have a hobby-horse, Mr Anderson?'

He did: wheat pennies. His greatest hope was to some day come across a 1955 double-date, which was—

But she knew that, too. The '55 double-date was a mistake. A valuable mistake.

Young Mr Anderson, he of the thick and carefully combed brown hair, was delighted with this answer. He asked her to call him Bob. Later, during their lunch – which they took on a bench in the sunshine behind the body shop, a tuna on rye for him and a Greek salad in a Tupperware bowl for her – he asked if she would like to go with him on Saturday to a street sale in Castle Rock. He had just rented a new apartment, he said, and was looking for an armchair. Also a TV, if someone was selling a good one at a fair price. *A good one at a fair price* was a phrase with which she would grow comfortably familiar in the years to come.

He was as plain as she was, just another guy you'd pass on the street without noticing, and would never have makeup to make him prettier . . . except that day on the bench, he did. His cheeks flushed when he asked her out, just enough to light him up a little and give him a glow.

'No coin collections?' she teased.

He smiled, revealing even teeth. Small teeth, nicely cared for, and white. It never occurred to her that the thought of those teeth could make her shudder – why would it?

'If I saw a nice set of coins, of course I'd look,' he said.

'Especially wheat pennies?' Teasing, but just a little.

'Especially those. Would you like to come, Darcy?'

She came. And she came on their wedding night, too. Not terribly often after that, but now and then. Often enough to consider herself normal and fulfilled.

In 1986, Bob got a promotion. He also (with Darcy's encouragement and help) started up a small mail-order business in collectible American coins. It was successful from the start, and in 1990, he added baseball trading cards and old movie memorabilia. He kept no stock of posters, one-sheets, or window cards, but when people queried him on such items, he could almost always find them. Actually it was Darcy who found them, using her over-stuffed Rolodex in those pre-computer days to call collectors all over the country. The business never got big enough to become full-time, and that was all right. Neither of them wanted such a thing. They agreed on that as they did on the house they eventually bought in Pownal, and on the children when it came time to have them. They agreed. When they didn't agree, they compromised. But mostly they agreed. They saw eye-to-eye.

How's your marriage?

It was good. A good marriage. Donnie was born in 1986 – she quit her job to have him, and except for helping with Anderson Coins & Collectibles never held another one – and Petra was born in 1988. By then, Bob Anderson's thick brown hair was thinning at the crown, and by 2002, the year Darcy's Macintosh computer finally swallowed her Rolodex whole, he had a large shiny bald spot back there. He experimented with different ways of combing what was left, which only made the bald spot more conspicuous, in her opinion. And he irritated her by trying two of the magical grow-it-all-back formulas, the kind of stuff sold by shifty-looking hucksters on high cable late at night (Bob Anderson became something of a night owl as he slipped into middle age). He didn't tell her he'd done it, but they shared a bedroom and although she wasn't tall enough to see the top shelf of the closet unaided, she some-times used a stool to put away his 'Saturday shirts,' the tees he wore for puttering in the garden. And there they were: a bottle of liquid in the fall of 2004, a bottle of little green gel capsules a year later. She looked the names up on the Internet, and they weren't cheap. *Of course magic never is*, she remembered thinking.

But, irritated or not, she had held her peace about the magic potions, and also about the used Chevy Suburban he for some reason just had to buy in the same year that gas prices really started to climb. As he had held his, she supposed (as she *knew*, actually), when she had insisted on good summer camps for the kids, an electric guitar for Donnie (he had played for two years, long enough to get surprisingly good, and then had simply stopped), horse rentals for Petra. A successful marriage was a balancing act – that was a thing everyone knew. A successful marriage was also dependent on a high tolerance for irritation – this was a thing *Darcy* knew. As the Stevie Winwood song said, you had to roll widdit, baby.

She rolled with it. So did he.

In 2004, Donnie went off to college in Pennsylvania. In 2006, Petra went to Colby, just up the road in Waterville. By then, Darcy Madsen Anderson was forty-six years old. Bob was forty-nine, and still doing Cub Scouts with Stan Morin, a construction contractor who lived half a mile down the road. She thought her balding husband looked rather amusing in the khaki shorts and long brown socks he wore for the monthly Wildlife Hikes, but never said so. His bald spot had become well entrenched; his glasses had become bifocals; his weight had spun up from one-eighty into the two-twenty range. He had become a partner in the accounting firm – Benson and Bacon was now Benson, Bacon & Anderson. They had traded the starter home in Pownal for a more expensive one in Yarmouth. Her breasts, formerly small and firm and high (her best feature, she'd always thought; she'd never wanted to look like a Hooters waitress), were now larger, not so firm, and of course they dropped down when she took off her bra at night – what else could you expect when you were closing in on the half-century mark? – but every so often Bob would still come up behind her and cup them. Every so often there was the pleasant interlude in the upstairs bedroom overlooking their peaceful two-acre patch of land, and if he was a little quick on the draw and often left her unsatisfied, often was not always, and the satisfaction of holding him afterwards, feeling his warm man's body as he drowsed away next to her . . . that satisfaction never failed. It was, she supposed, the satisfaction of knowing they were still together when so many others were not; the satisfaction of knowing that as they approached their Silver Anniversary, the course was still steady as she goes.

In 2009, twenty-five years down the road from their I-do's in a small Baptist church that no longer existed (there was now a parking lot where it had stood), Donnie and Petra threw them a surprise party at The Birches on Castle View. There were over fifty guests, champagne (the good stuff), steak tips, a four-tier cake. The honorees danced to Kenny Loggins's 'Footloose,' just as they had at their wedding. The guests applauded Bob's breakaway move, one she had forgotten until she saw it again, and its still-airy execution gave her a pang. Well it should have; he had grown a paunch to go with the embarrassing bald spot (embarrassing to him, at least), but he was still extremely light on his feet for an accountant.

But all of that was just history, the stuff of obituaries, and they were still too young to be thinking of those. It ignored the minutiae of marriage, and such ordinary mysteries, she believed (*firmly* believed), were the stuff that validated the partnership. The time she had eaten bad shrimp and vomited all night long, sitting on the edge of the bed with her sweaty hair clinging to the nape of her neck and tears rolling down her flushed cheeks and Bob sitting beside her, patiently holding the basin and then taking it to the bathroom, where he emptied and rinsed it after each ejection – so the smell of it wouldn't make her even sicker, he said. He had been warming up the car to take her to the Emergency Room at six the next morning when the horrible nausea had finally begun to abate. He had called in sick at B, B & A; he'd also canceled a trip to White River so he could sit with her in case the sickness came back.

That kind of thing worked both ways; one year's sauce for the goose was next year's sauce for the gander. She had sat with him in the waiting room at St Stephen's – back in '94 or '95, this had been – waiting for the biopsy results after he had discovered (in the shower) a suspicious lump in his left armpit. The biopsy had been negative, the diagnosis an infected lymph node. The lump had lingered for another month or so, then went away on its own.

The sight of a crossword book on his knees glimpsed through the half-open bathroom door as he sat on the commode. The smell of cologne on his cheeks, which meant that the Suburban would be gone from the driveway for a day or two and his side of the bed would be empty for a night or two because he had to straighten out someone's accounting in New Hampshire or Vermont (B, B & A now had clients in all the northern New England states). Sometimes the smell meant a trip to look at someone's coin collection at an estate sale, because not all the numismatic buying and selling that went with their side-business could be accomplished by computer, they both understood that. The sight of his old black suitcase, the one he would never give up no matter how much she nagged, in the front hall. His slippers at the end of the bed, one always tucked into the other. The glass of water on his endtable, with the orange vitamin pill next to it, on that month's issue of *Coin & Currency Collecting*. How he always said, 'More room out than there is in' after belching and 'Look out, gas attack!' after he farted. His coat on the first hook in the hall. The reflection of his toothbrush in the mirror (he would still be using the same one he'd had when they got married, Darcy believed, if she didn't regularly replace it). The way he dabbed his lips with his napkin after every second or third bite of food. The careful arrangement of camping gear (always including an extra compass) before he and Stan set out with yet another bunch of nine-year-olds on the hike up Dead Man's Trail – a dangerous and terrifying trek that took them through the woods behind the Golden Grove Mall and came out at Weinberg's Used Car City. The look of his nails, always short and clean. The taste of Dentyne on his breath when they kissed. These things and ten thousand others comprised the secret history of the marriage.

She knew he must have his own history of her, everything from the cinnamon-flavored ChapStick she used on her lips in the winter to the smell of her shampoo when he nuzzled the back of her neck (that nuzzle didn't come so often now, but it still came) to the click of her computer at two in the morning on those two or three nights a month when sleep for some reason jilted her.

Now it was twenty-seven years, or – she had amused herself figuring this one day using the calculator function on her computer – nine thousand, eight hundred and fifty-five days. Almost a quarter of a million hours and over fourteen million minutes. Of course some of that time he'd been gone on business, and she'd taken a few trips herself (the saddest to be with her parents in Minneapolis after her kid sister Brandolyn had died in a freak accident), but mostly they had been together.

Did she know everything about him? Of course not. No more than he knew everything about her – how she sometimes (mostly on rainy days or on those nights when the insomnia was on her) gobbled Butterfingers or Baby Ruths, for instance, eating the candybars even after she no longer wanted them, even after she felt sick to her stomach. Or how she thought the new mailman was sort of cute. There was no knowing everything, but she felt that after twenty-seven years, they knew all the important things. It was a good marriage, one of the fifty percent or so that kept working over the long haul. She believed that in the same unquestioning way she believed that gravity would hold her to the earth when she walked down the sidewalk.

Until that night in the garage.

CARRIE

First came the blood.
Then came the power.

'Guaranteed to chill you' – *The New York Times*

'One of the great storytellers of our time'
– *Guardian*

HODDER

MISERY

He's a famous writer.
She's his number one fan.

'The greatest popular novelist of our day'
– *Guardian*

'[One of] Stephen King's best . . . Genuinely scary'
– *USA Today*

HODDER

STEPHEN KING

ROSE MADDER

She's on the run.
But he'll never let her go.

'A superb suspense novel' – *The Sunday Times*

'Relentlessly paced and brilliantly orchestrated'
– *Publishers Weekly*

HODDER

To find out more about Stephen King please visit
www.hodder.co.uk, www.stephenkingbooks.co.uk,
www.facebook.com/stephenkingbooks